I0708318

DARK SIDE

LARRYALEXANDER

Phyllis Emmert

Illustrator

phyllisemmert.com

Introduction

Okay, okay. I know what I said in the introduction of *Half Moon*. And I paraphrase "is there going to be a sequel to *Half Moon*? The answer would be no. I'm so tired of making crap up."

Unfortunately, I still wake up most nights about 3:00 a.m. and once again I needed something constructive to think about until I fell back to sleep, so here is the sequel to *Half Moon*. Besides, *Half Moon* was so lucrative. It sold sixty-eight copies world-wide so far; five in Germany and one in Bermuda.

The other thing is the extraterrestrials kind of grow on you. It was hard to let them go. My sister-in-law, Linda, said that the ETs kind of became family to her. She was sorry to see them leave at the end in *Half Moon*.

So, here we go. The adventures continue for Mike, Kate, and the ETs in *Dark Side*.

DARK SIDE

Larry Alexander

1

Autumn at Pine Creek was almost enchanting. Morning temperatures were crisp with occasional frost that highlighted the contours of the surrounding hills. Afternoons became warm accented by clean valley scents. Colors were changing. Wild Rose trees were turning a vibrant deep red along with the sumac. Bunches of rabbit brush and serviceberry bushes became lemon yellow. Groves of quaking aspen leaves shimmered with an almost yellow, neon quality in the winds as the leaves eventually fell to the ground fluttering like large yellow-orange snowflakes. Along with ponderosa pine trees, they all dotted the hillsides in amongst the brown bunch grass; fall patches of color creating a valley tapestry.

The creek itself gurgled along really not in a hurry to go anywhere. No longer the torrents of last spring, little pools of water had formed over the summer as the creek slowly made its way south. Various grasses and weeds had grown up along the creek's banks. From our home up above, it looked like a large green snake slowly crawling through the brown meadow. Whether the creek would run all winter depended on last winter's snowfall.

As Pine Creek slowed, so did the traffic. There really wasn't much anyway, just the usual locals going somewhere. Now that hunting season was officially over the occasional road hunters had left.

I sipped my coffee while sitting in the oak rocking chair looking out of our picture windows to the valley below. I watched our four black Angus steers meander up to where they were grained every day. They looked in the empty feed trays and then gazed over at the road leading to the pasture. Yeah, I needed to get down there to feed the steers their grain. Every spring our neighbor would go to the cattle auction in Okanogan and buy four young black Angus steers for us. They would keep the grass down in our pasture all spring and summer. Then come October we would grain them for a month to add some marbling of fat in the steers' muscle. And the eventual butchering of the steers would take place. The Langendorf brothers ran the local butcher business. Ben would cut and wrap the meat while brother Don traveled to farms and pastures slaughtering the animals. Don was a husky man in his early forties and somewhat mischievous. Kate always dreaded this time of year because inevitably she was the one who had to meet Don in the pasture and grain the steers for the last time to bring them in. Then before she could get in our Chevy Blazer to drive back up the driveway, Kate would hear four quick cracks from Don's .22 rifle.

Kate decided that last fall would be different. She met Don where the steers were fed, but told him not to shoot before she got in the SUV. After she had fed the steers, Kate turned around and briskly walked back to our Blazer. Before she could grab the door handle, Don dropped all four steers chuckling as he did. Pretty funny, I thought, as I began to put my sneakers on.

I drank the last of my coffee as I saw the school bus round the corner and travel by our property on the county road. Soon it drove out of site. About twenty years ago Joel, our youngest son at fourteen years old, was coming home on the school bus. It stopped by our mailbox, but Joel didn't get off. We knew Ronnie, the bus driver, very well. She was in her early sixties with flaming red hair and lipstick to match. It was her husband who would buy the steers for us. Chris would often ride horses with Ronnie on trail rides up in the surrounding hills. Ronnie was originally from Issaquah, a small city next to Bellevue by Seattle. She and her husband had operated their 100-acre ranch for the past forty years just a few miles below us. Somehow her west coast accent had slowly developed into a Texas drawl over the years here east of the mountains.

Anyway, the school bus sat there for several minutes. I thought to myself, geez, was Joel in trouble for something he had done on the bus? After ten minutes or so, he finally stepped off the bus and walked up our driveway. When he came in the house I asked him why he was on the bus for so long? He explained that Ronnie just want-ed to talk to him about how things were going at school and asked questions about other students. Ronnie loved gossip. Joel said the last thing she asked was, "What's the deal with that Stu Bledsoe?" We both had to laugh at that one.

Yep, autumn was almost enchanting. It just meant that winter would soon be here.

I got up out of the rocking chair and walked into the kitchen to refill my coffee cup. Suddenly, the dogs began barking. Their constant barks were loud, sharp, and fierce. What has got them so worked up, I wondered? The last time they sounded like that there was a huge black bear lumbering its way up the rocky hill in front of our house. This time the barking was coming from the back of our home where our long gravel driveway came up from Pine Creek Road. I hurried from the kitchen and around the end of the counter where Kate's half a cup of coffee was still sitting. She was subbing today in kindergarten at the local elementary school and had gotten a little behind getting ready. She had left in a hurry.

I went to the picture windows in the living room and looked out. Slowly coming up our driveway were three black SUVs. What was the deal with this, I wondered? I put down my coffee. This didn't feel right at all. I left the living room and walked across the entry to the front door. I saw my wallet and truck keys sitting in their usual spot in a basket on a small table by the front door. You know, I thought, I'd better put my wallet in my pants back pocket.

As I opened the front door the dogs rushed over to me. They were extremely agitated. This was not how they acted when people would come to visit. Visitors always claimed that the dogs would lick them to death, instead of being good watch dogs. I shushed the dogs and motioned for them to get in back of me. Just then the three black Chevy Suburbans came slowly around the aspen grove and into view. The white U.S. government license plates stood out from the polished black SUVs; not so shiny anymore after coming up our dusty gravel driveway. They came to a halt by the front lawn and sidewalk. Dust swirled around the vehicles creating an eerie atmosphere to the already surreal scene.

Almost simultaneously, the two front doors of the Suburbans opened. The driver and passenger stepped out and closed their doors. Each driver walked around the vehicles and stood by the passenger. They were all young men except for a woman by the last Suburban. They all appeared to be in their thirties and forties. Each one was dressed in a dark gray suit with white shirts and matching gray ties.

The passenger of the second SUV began walking towards our house on the sidewalk to the front door. The dogs began a low growl as the man approached. I tried to calm them with some thought talk.

The young man was tall with an expression of intensity. He had short brown hair and his strong jaw was closely shaven. He was physically fit and moved with a self-assured stride. I stood on the top step. He came up and stood on the step below in front of me. Our heights were now even as I looked into his steel-blue eyes.

"Mr. McAlister? Mr. Michael McAlister?" he asked in a soft, confident voice.

Still staring into his eyes, I finally asked, "Who wants to know?"

"United States Government Reserves Unit In Tactical Security", he said as he lifted the left side of his jacket coat revealing some kind of blue-gold-silver badge attached to his pants' belt. He then firmly gripped the back of my left arm and began pulling me off the front porch. "This is an urgent matter of national security. You need to come with us immediately."

I jerked my arm free. "Do you mind if I close the front door first?" I said firmly. Turning around, I shut the door and made a decision. It took just three seconds to find out it was a poor one. I came back around to face the young man still standing on the second step. I delivered a left jab to his chiseled jaw, followed by a right cross landing on his left cheek, and a left hook to his right eye. Before I could hit his chin with an upper-cut, I experienced a stinging sensation on my upper right arm. Immediately, the feeling of a thousand bald-faced hornets stinging me under my skin enveloped me as 30,000 volts jolted my body. All my muscles locked up and I fell on the porch landing. My arms and legs began to convulse as I heard a calm, authoritative voice say, "Doctor, if you please..." As my consciousness began fading away to darkness, I saw the figures of Bill and Sammie laying down on the lawn convulsing, too.

2

The sedation wore off. I woke up and opened my eyes. Black. Everywhere was black. Geez, not this again. I soon realized though that there were differences than being in the black void with the librarian. I felt vibrations, movements and gravity. I was sitting down. It became apparent there was a seat belt holding me up vertically in a moving vehicle. Evidently I had a black hood on my head. I tried to remain calm and pretended to still be asleep. If I listened carefully, I thought, perhaps I could gain some knowledge about my current situation, whatever that was.

From the noise outside of the vehicle, we were driving on a gravel road. The driver wasn't speaking and neither were any passengers. I moved my wrists a little to feel if I was bound by a rope or handcuffs. It felt like all my muscles were stiff and sore. If I flexed my fingers a touch...oh, my god! I could barely move them. They were stiff, swollen, and extremely sore. I had forgotten about hitting the young man in the gray suit.

The huge impact of the explosion under the vehicle was sudden, unexpected and violent. It felt like the vehicle was catapulted off of the ground about five feet in the air. I was thrown upwards as the vehicle slammed back down, tipping over on its left side. My head slammed against the glass window of the vehicle door. Temporarily unconscious, I came to hearing explosions all around us. Each one rocked our vehicle. Pop-pop-pop-pop-pop-pop-pop. It sounded like bullets from gunfire were hitting all sides of the vehicle I was in.

"Hawk 1 and Hawk 3, Hawk 2. We are disabled. Olsen is either unconscious or dead. Hawk 1, status, over." I thought, that voice; calm, commanding, authoritative. It came from the front seat of this vehicle's cab!

"We are able and ready to engage the hostile force. They have four vehicles, one disabled, over"

"Hawk 3, status, over.

"We are able and ready to engage the hostile force, over."

"Hawk 1 and Hawk 3, Hawk 2. Engage hostile forces with conventional weapons on each target while readying and launching the drones. When the drones are in position and locked on the enemy targets, launch the missiles, over."

"Hawk 1, wilco, over."

"Hawk 3, wilco, over."

"Roger, out"

Whoever was giving orders was assured, single-minded, and articulate. At that instance came four huge explosions, one sending our vehicle sliding sideways scraping on the gravel road and down into a small ravine. We soon stopped with a sudden thud rocking the vehicle back and forth on its top. I was hanging upside-down supported by the seat belt. The enormous sounds and repercussions of the exploding missiles into the hostile forces' vehicles left me deafened and disoriented.

"Hawk 2, Hawk 1. The hostile forces' vehicles are destroyed, over."

"Hawk 1 and Hawk 3, Hawk 2. Excellent execution. Rendezvous with Hawk 2 and retrieve Olsen, me and the hostage, over."

Hostage!? How did I become a hostage? I had been assaulted, kidnapped, and held against my will for who knows how long. Maybe that is why he called me a hostage. But why me and to what end?

I walked with the assistance of two people, one on each side clutching my arms. The black hood was still in place. It seemed we had walked a long ways together. By the sounds of our steps reverberating off the walls, it was a very long hallway. Eventually we stopped. A door was opened and I entered to my right side. They took me to a chair and I was seated. I could hear a key entering a lock next to my neck and the black hood was lifted off. The light was blinding and I tightly closed my eyes.

A woman's voice said, "Gradually open your eyes." She and her partner left and locked the door behind them. It was painful getting used to my new surroundings. Similar to having your eyes dilated during an eye exam, then you step outside the examination room into sunshine. When I felt my eyes were ready, I squinted looking around the small room. No bigger than twelve by twelve feet, the walls, ceiling and floor were painted a brilliant white. I was seated by a table with another chair on the other side. They were all white, too. No windows, no two-way mirrors. There was a cot next to the wall behind me; standard military issue with a blanket and small pillow. However, there was a TV camera in the corner ahead of my right shoulder. I was alone. I also had to urinate.

I looked around deciding which corner I was going to use when the door opened and two men in gray suits entered. The first man was tall sporting aviator Ray Bans. Behind the glasses looked like purplish-blue bruises. The other man was also tall, maybe late thirties, black hair with an earbud in his left ear. Handsome wasn't the word, but maybe rugged good looks described his facial features. The way he comported himself left no doubt who was in charge. He pulled the chair out from under the table. It didn't make a sound as it slid on the floor. He sat down opposite me and put both arms on the table folding his hands together. As he sat, his posture was perfectly straight. He carried no file folder, no envelope, and no paperwork; just himself and his assistant.

"Hello, Mr. McCalister." The voice! He was the man that coordinated the counter-offensive against whoever attacked us in the three vehicles! "You have met my assistant Steve," as his head tilted to his right. "My compliments. No one catches Steve off his guard." I decided to keep my eyes looking directly into the man's eyes seated across from me. I didn't want to make eye contact with Steve in case he held a grudge.

"Our interest in you stems from these facts. You have been to the moon. Not only to the moon, but inside the moon. You know, it took Apollo crews three days to reach the moon. You accomplished this feat in just three minutes."

"Then you went back in time to 1989." He paused for several moments. How does this guy know these things, I thought? There is absolutely no way he could be aware of all this, no way! I kept staring into his vibrant green eyes. "Any comments?" he asked.

"Yes. I've got to take a piss."

He looked to his upper left as his right hand pressed against his earbud. His expression did not change as he stood up and told his assistant, "Please see to it that Mr. McAlister is taken to a latrine," and abruptly left the room.

I was led to a bathroom by Steve and a woman that joined us

in the white hallway. She fit the same description as the men. Wearing a gray suit, she had shoulder length brown hair, and was physically fit. Her expression was one of intensity and resolve. Standing by the bathroom they motioned for me to go inside. The bathroom had a lone stall, a shower, one sink, and a urinal. Relieving myself, I began thinking about how much more these people could know about me and the ETs, the moon's Crystals, and even the librarian. Really, there was absolutely no way they could, but here I was held captive by some government or military entity. Or perhaps something else...

As I washed my hands I looked into the mirror above the sink. Wow, I did not look so good. My hair was all goofed up, I had at least a days' beard stubble on my face, and there were dark circles under my eyes. A huge purplish-red knot stood out on the left side of my forehead. Everything had happened so fast. I don't even know how long I have been abducted. I thought about Kate and what she must be thinking. I mean, I have totally disappeared. She and I have no idea when or where I am.

I opened the bathroom door and stepped out into the hallway. Steve and the young woman were gone. I looked up and down the hallway. There was no one present. What the heck is going on? Is escape from this place, wherever it is, now possible?

Since Steve and the woman pivoted me from right to left in front of the bathroom door, I decided to continue in the opposite direction. Just like the interrogation room, the hallway walls were a brilliant white. I walked at a swift pace stopping every once in a while listening for pursuers. Occasionally I would come upon a door. I tried the doorknobs, but all were locked. After what seemed like ten minutes, I came to an elevator door at the end of the hallway. There was only one button by it. I pushed it and to my surprise, the elevator door swiftly opened.

Inside the elevator car was a vertical row of ten buttons, none labeled. Well, let's go to the top and see what happens, I thought. I pushed the top button. The car wasted no time getting to the top floor. The elevator door opened. I gasped at what I saw. I was standing by a city street. The skies were gray with a gentle, cool mist falling. I was not dressed for this weather at all. Off in the distance I saw huge mountains partially covered with snow. The mountain tops were hidden by dark, gray clouds. Everywhere I looked were light brown, two story rectangular buildings with gently sloped metal roofs. They all looked exactly the same. It had to be a military base. But where was I? I heard a clap of thunder off in the distance.

A yellow taxi drove up on the street in front of me. Wow, what luck! I waved my hand and the taxi pulled over and stopped right in front of me. Could it be this easy? I opened the passenger door. "Where to?" the cabbie asked. He seemed like a typical cab driver. He was middle-aged, greasy black hair, and sporting a goatee. His black nose hairs were so thick and long that they may be contributing to his mustache. There were two large signs inside his cab; one on the dash and another on the ceiling above the rear view mirror. In big black letters they said "NO SMOKING." Once again, there was a clap of thunder, closer this time.

"First though," I asked, "where are we?" The cab driver looked at me with frowning black eyebrows. "Maybe you need to shut the door and back away."

"No, no wait. I'll double your tip, just tell me where I am?" More thunder and it was getting closer. There was also the sound of gunfire. Was there a shooting range close by?

"Okay, but no trouble from you. Specifically, you are on Elmendorf Air Force Base by the front gates. Generally, you're in Anchorage." After a hesitation, "Alaska."

I sat there a moment thinking of the implications. An explosion took place to my left and I could see a ball of fire and smoke just beyond the buildings. Gunfire was now persistent and sounded like it was just yards away. There was another explosion with some debris falling close to where the taxi cab and I were located. "Can you get me to Ted Stevens Airport?"

"Yes, sir!"

As I climbed in the back seat of the cab, I could see bullets hitting into the siding just above the elevator door leaving holes and wood splinters flying everywhere. As we tore out of the base, the cab driver asked, "Do you mind if I smoke?"

We arrived at Departure. I paid the fee and generously tipped the cab driver. With a hearty thank you, he sped off. You know, I thought, my capture was smart, efficient, and knowledgeable about tactics. But somehow I have escaped. And more importantly, I still have my wallet. Okay, I want to get home.

I walked through the airport doors and looked at the signs above: Baggage downstairs, Security Check-in straight ahead and Alaska Airlines Ticketing to the right. Okay, I thought, get my airline ticket, get to Seattle and then figure out my way back to Pine Creek in Tonasket. With resolve, I turned towards ticketing and began walking. I could see the familiar blue and white Alaska Airlines sign several feet ahead. Then I abruptly stopped. In front of me were four men in gray suits. I quickly turned around and there were four more gray-suited men behind me. My shoulders slumped acknowledging failure. How do these guys seemingly know where I am all the time?

3

Once more I found myself seated in a chair with the black hood being taken off my head. I was somewhat groggy after being sedated again. When my eyes became accustomed to the light, it appeared I was in the same interrogation room as before. I sat behind a small rectangular table with a similar chair on the other side. Except this room had three TV monitors next to the ceiling on the wall that I faced. The door swung open and in strode 'The Voice' along with a gray-suited man; young, fit with the intensity look. This time the Voice carried a file-folder.

He sat down in the chair across from me. "I apologize for the sedation. It is however, in your best interest and safety," 'The Voice' explained. He carefully opened the folder. He stared at a photograph for a moment. "Mr. McAlister, perhaps evidence of your trip to the moon and time travel may jog your memory." He turned the photo around and slid it over in front of me.

"On May of this year you spent time inside St. Peter's Lutheran Church on Whidbey Island. It was in the evening and you turned the lights on in the sanctuary. A neighbor saw the lights in the church and went outside to investigate. He took this photograph of you entering an unidentified flying object." He sat there staring at me, I'm sure, hoping for a full confession. After an uncomfortable amount of time I asked, "Who am I addressing?"

"Commander Logan," he answered.

"Commander Logan, I see a somewhat blurry picture of the backside of some person standing below the glow of a street lamp. It could be a picture of anyone."

Commander Logan produced another document from the file folder, turned it around and slid it over to me. "These are your fingerprints on the door handle in the back of the church and on the light switch in the sanctuary." I continued to stare at him trying not to look surprised. A fuzzy photo, my fingerprints, but how does this Logan

19

know I went to the moon? And how could he possibly know about going back to 1989?

"Because of the photo and fingerprints," he began, "we became curious. Soon we tracked you, not just going to the moon, but inside the moon. Then you traveled back in time to your former residence at Ponderosa Estates in eastern Washington. You were there approximately twelve minutes. At that point you became a national security issue of the highest priority."

How on earth does he know this stuff, I thought? Maybe it wasn't on earth. Were the ETs providing Logan with information about me? No, that just didn't seem possible.

"I'm starving," I said. Commander Logan looked at the man to his right. He left the room as another gray suit came in and took his place standing next to Commander Logan.

"You are reluctant to talk to me about these events. Eventually you will. But first, let me tell you what has been taking place. We survived the first assault together in the SUV caravan. Then there was another altercation at Elmendorf Air Force Base. And currently we have just pushed back another attack."

The news of the attacks was incredulous. "Who is doing this to us?" I demanded.

"Some are foreign nationals, and some are their own foreign entities with no national affiliations. You are extremely fortunate that we arrived at your home first. Somehow because of your unique abilities, the word has gotten out. We are not the only ones with high intelligence gathering capabilities. As they say," and he paused, "you have become a hot commodity."

"Just what branch of the United Sates military do you command?" I asked.

Commander Logan replied, "The United States Government Reserves Unit in Tactical Security."

"You must have an acronym shortening the name of your military branch," I inquired.

"We call ourselves Gruits."

I pressed on. "And what's with all the gray suits?"

"It is our uniform," Commander Logan stated.

Gruits, I thought. And then it hit me; Gruits, gray suits, Gruits. You've got to be kidding me. With some sarcasm, I asked, "Did you have a contest and someone won a prize thinking that up?"

As Logan just stared at me, my lunch arrived. The sandwich consisted of whole wheat bread, turkey, Swiss cheese, lettuce, and mayonnaise. It was accompanied with a glass of water. As I took a couple bites, I wondered about Kate, where she was and was she safe? I desperately wanted to ask Logan these questions, but thought that if I did, somehow she might become involved. Commander Logan stood up and said, "I will leave you to your meal. What I need to know are two things: how do you travel to the moon in three minutes and how do you accomplish time travel? I will be back soon." As Logan left the man to his right pivoted smartly and followed. I finished my sandwich, put my head in my arms on the table and tried to sleep a little.

The interrogation room door opened. Startled, I woke up. I turned towards the door ready to engage Commander Logan in a debate about an American citizen being held hostage against his will. Where were my unalienable rights guaranteed by the Constitution? As I spun around to face Logan, I was shocked at what I saw.

Standing in the door frame staring at me was an ET; but not one of my ETs. This ET had a reddish tinge to it, like it had been out in the sun a little too long. ~Follow me~, it thought. I got up and followed it through the door and into the hallway. Suddenly, I felt somewhat hopeful about my situation.

Following behind the ET, I noticed a little limp to its gait, almost like a skip every time it took a step. Maybe this guy was one of the ETs first attempts at the ET reproduction process. Perhaps they were practicing on this poor guy. We came to elevator doors, similar to the ones at Elmendorf. We stepped in and quickly took off to the top; no button pushing required.

~Hey, uh, Sundance. What is going on?~

~We are providing a means of escape from your current situation. All surveillance devices have been temporarily neutralized. Our craft is waiting up above to transport you to any destination of your choosing.~

Finally, I thought, finally! I was no longer going to be held hostage by Logan and his minions. This feels so good! A moment ago I was desolate; now I am ecstatic. We stepped out of the elevator car into brilliant sunshine. The air was hot, dry and felt wonderful. There was even a floral scent giving the moment of freedom a warming sensation. I scanned the horizon. There were jagged, rocky mountains all around with little to no vegetation on them. We were not in Anchorage anymore. Eerily similar to Elmendorf Air Force Base, the buildings were two-story, square and rectangular with gently slopped roofs. The building colors were all painted a drab brown.

I followed Sundance around the corner of a large building, perhaps a hanger. There were several of these buildings all in a row. Sundance was still skipping and hopping as it walked along. Suddenly Sundance's craft lowered in front of us. As I stripped off my clothes, Sundance entered its craft. I soon followed. Oh, that feeling of warmth and comfort inside the ship's medium had a soothing sensation. I looked around. Three more ETs were present and everything looked exactly the same as if Rosie and the guys were here.

~What is your destination?~ Sundance asked.

~First, I want to go home and check in with Kate and the dogs. Then after that, the moon.~

Immediately their ship shot upward. And then suddenly stopped. I looked at Sundance. ~Problem?~

~A web-like dome of extremely intense electro-magnetic frequency waves has been quickly put in place over and around the entire area where you were being held.~

~Can we go through it?~

~We can,~ thought Sundance. ~You cannot. You would not survive.~

How does Logan do this? Somehow he knows my every move. Sundance said the surveillance equipment had been temporarily taken out. No one witnessed me leaving the interrogation room. Unless I can figure out how the Commander does this, I am doomed.

We returned to where we had just taken off. My clothes were still on the ground. As I began dressing I asked it how I could make contact in the future. Sundance thought, ~I will contact you~. And then I asked, ~Where are Rosie, Satchmo, Lumpy, and James T?~ No response.

As easy as it was to escape, it was just as easy getting back to the interrogation room. I sat down in the chair and put my head on my arms resting on the table, totally dejected.

"Hello, Mr. McAlister. Mr. McAlister, hello." I woke up, slowly lifted my head off of the table and found Commander Logan sitting across from me in the interrogation room. I looked around the room and back to Logan. Nothing had changed, except seeing the commander again was somewhat comforting. That's odd, I thought. Standing next to him on his right was a man in the usual gray suit, but he was a little different than the others. For one thing, he appeared somewhat older. Still fit, he was mostly bald with some gray hair on his head that was combed straight back.

"Mr. McAlister, may I call you Mike?" I nodded my head. "First, I want to point out how extremely lucky you have been since we arrived at your home before any foreign nationals or extremists groups did. Since we acquired you we have been attacked three times, each one being repelled successfully. Even though you are in my custody, the United States government and specifically the United States military, are protecting you. You are completely safe." He paused for a moment I'm sure, to let these facts sink in.

I looked again to the man on Logan's right. He looked vaguely familiar. I couldn't quite place where but it seemed that I had met him before.

"Mike, it is of the utmost importance for the United States' security that we..."

"Excuse me, Commander Logan," I interjected, "And how may I address you?"

Logan stopped talking for a moment and finally said, "Ryan."

"Thank you Ryan. I know that you want to secure this information for the sake of the United States, how I accomplish going to the moon and travel back in time." I stopped talking. There was an odd sound in the interrogation room. I looked around trying to discover the source of the noise. No wait, there it was again. It was a familiar sound! The man in the gray suit next to Ryan was jingling change in his pants pocket.

"Bill, please..." Logan said looking at Bill's pants pocket.

"Sorry, sir," Bill replied.

His voice, I thought. I recognized his voice. Suddenly, memories began flooding back to me. My god! I know this man! He was at the bed and breakfast that morning in Green Lake talking to me!

4

It's one thing to welcome the kindergartners into the classroom in the morning before school starts. It was another making sure each student got on the correct bus going home. With a sheet of paper that listed all the student's names and corresponding bus numbers from the protocol folder, Kate had just delivered the last of the kindies to the correct bus. She began walking up the bus row and back to the kindergarten classroom.

"Hey Kate, how'd ya'll do in kindergarten today?" The familiar voice of Ronnie. Kate stopped and looked through the open bus door. There was Ronnie sitting in the driver's seat soon to be driving her bus route.

Kate said, "I had a great day of singing, dancing, coloring, reading, and laughing with five and six years olds. The only small concern was Timmy who insisted he was not going to participate in dancing to music. I told him that was fine. Instead, he could watch us seated at a table across the room. When he was ready to rejoin the class, he could just walk over and do so. I think he sat about a minute before he slid into the middle of his classmates and joined in."

"That Tim," Ronnie said, " what a pistol. But I think he has a good heart. So, we ridin' this weekend?"

"I'm looking forward to it. When do you want to go?" Kate asked.

"If it works for you, I'll pick you and Babe up about 9:00 a.m. Saturday morning."

"Thanks Ronnie, Babe and I will be ready waiting down by the mailbox," Kate said.

"Great, see ya then," Ronnie said with a big smile on her face with the signature red lipstick.

As Kate walked back to the classroom she thought how lucky she was to have such a good friend like Ronnie. She and Babe would get picked up in Ronnie's Ford diesel one-ton truck and horse trailer. Then they would drive up in the hills and find a place to park and unload. They always had a great time riding the hills around the Pine Creek area, thought Kate.

She walked into the kindergarten classroom and began straightening up the room so it was custodial ready. She wrote notes to the regular teacher of the day's highlights and told her she had a great day with her class. Kate put her coat on and grabbed her purse. As she walked to the school parking lot, she thought the day was going to get even better. Mike had promised he would be cooking her a special dinner tonight and there would be a glass of chardonnay waiting for her on the kitchen counter when she arrived home.

It didn't take much to get to the McAlister residence from school. Out of the school parking lot, you took a right onto Highway 20, then merged right on Highway 97, and then quickly turned left by the hardware store. After negotiating the four-way stop and crossing the river over the 5th street bridge, you turned left onto Highway 7. The next right you entered Pine Creek Road. From school, it took about three minutes depending on light to no traffic. Now it was nine more miles up a somewhat windy road until you got to the McAlister home. Along the way you would drive through three beautiful and picturesque valleys through the surrounding mountains. Elevation in town was about 900 feet. But when you reached the McAlisters, it turned into 2,550 feet; cooler summers, but cold and snowy winters.

Kate drove the windy road by the trout farm and then reached the second valley. Soon Ronnie and Lee's ranch was in full view off to the left: a two-story farmhouse, three barns, and several out-buildings stuffed with tools and farm equipment. All of these buildings were surrounded by three large hay fields about eight acres each. The back of their place was bordered with large ponderosa pines. After driving half a mile you lost sight of Ronnie and Lee's ranch. There was still one more hill to climb until you reached McCalister's little valley.

Upon arriving home Kate put the Blazer in the garage and called the dogs. Usually when she stepped out of the SUV they would be right on her heels, but not today. She walked out to the front lawn to see where they were. She called their names. From the barn, they eventually came, not running, but walking; no hopping, no jumping waiting to get some attention after being home alone all day. Today they seemed quite lethargic and docile. That was odd, Kate thought. I'll be sure to talk to Mike about there strange behaviors.

After some petting Kate went back in the garage and through the door that entered the kitchen. She looked at the counter; no wine. In fact, where was Mike? He should be busy in the kitchen putting together a fabulous meal. Coming up the driveway she had seen that the truck was parked in the barn parking spot, so he had to be around somewhere.

"Mike," she called. Kate walked over to the downstairs staircase by the living room and called Mike again. No answer. Well, he must be doing something outside, she thought. She went out the front door and walked down towards the barn with Bill and Sammie close behind. She called Mike's name several times, but still no answer. She started to get a funny feeling about the whole situation.

Startling Kate, Bill and Sammie began barking. What is going on here, Kate thought? Just then three black Chevrolet Suburbans slowly drove around the corner of the aspen grove and pulled up by the front yard and sidewalk. Does this have something to do with Mike's disappearance, Kate wondered? She began walking up to the house where the three SUVs were waiting. As she stopped on the front lawn staring at the black Suburbans the dogs, whimpering and whining, headed for the garage and went inside. Another oddity, thought Kate. The dogs always liked greeting people as they got out of their vehicles. Kate watched as the driver and passenger stepped out of each SUV with the driver walking around the front and standing next to the passenger. All were men in their thirties, extremely fit and all wearing gray suits. The passenger of the second Suburban strode over to where Kate was standing. He stopped a comfortable distance away.

"Kathrine McAlister?" the young man asked.

"Yes, I am. And who are you?"

"I am Lieutenant Andrew Wright. I belong to a branch of the United States military."

"I would like to see your identification and how does this concern me?" Kate asked. Lieutenant Wright opened the left side of his gray coat revealing his blue, gold, and silver badge. Kate noticed some insignia on it and said, "Is this supposed to impress me? I want to see the identification in your wallet." Slowly, Lieutenant Wright reached inside the upper right of his jacket and produced his wallet and handed it to Kate. She opened it. The only thing it contained was his government-issue driver's license. The lieutenant's name and an address were on it. She handed it back and shrugged her shoulders.

"Mrs. McAlister, you and your husband's lives are in extreme danger. What I am allowed to tell you is this; your husband has exhibited two unique abilities that we recently became aware of. Mr. McAlister travels to the moon at astonishing speeds and can also go back in time." Kate was dumbfounded hearing this news from the lieutenant. How is it possible that they know this? "Unfortunately, the United States is not the only government that knows this," he continued. "Other governments, some friendly and some not, are aware of your husband's abilities, too. These could be foreign nationals, foreign entities, and possibly terrorist organizations who have also taken an interest in your husband's special talents."

"Everything you have said is absurd. What have you done with my husband?" Kate screamed!

The lieutenant shifted his weight to his left side and said, "Mr. McAilster is safe. Currently, he is with us at an undisclosed secure location. To emphasize, the danger to you and your husband is real. During transporting your husband early this afternoon to a secure location, we were attacked. The attack was repelled and everyone, including your husband, survived. We have yet to determine who the attackers were."

Kate felt light-headed. She turned around and walked over to the front porch steps and sat down. What is going on?! Staring at the lawn in front of her, she tried to sort everything all out. Mike is not here, she thought. These people, whoever they really are have taken Mike. He and I are in danger because of Mike's abilities to travel to the moon and back in time. Even though Mike was in a safe location they were attacked. And they think I may become a target, too. These people seem concerned about protecting me. But, I'm sure they must also want information from me about what Mike can do. What should I do, Kate thought?

With her head in her hands, Kate started to cry. Hearing this, Bill and Sammie looked around the garage corner. They slowly walked over and laid down next to her, one on either side. She looked at them through teary eyes and put her arms around both dogs. They were trembling. The lieutenant stood and watched. Finally, in a low voice, Kate said, "I will go with you, but I need an hour to get things

sorted out and taken care of here."

"Of course," the lieutenant said, "We will wait for you here."

5

"Mike, you were saying?" asked Commander Logan. I snapped out of my thoughts about the man from Green Lake that was standing right in front of me. Logan appeared to be frustrated and losing patience.

"Commander Logan, Ryan, I need more time, please."

Logan stood up. "Time is of the essence and we are running short". He and the man from Green Lake left the room.

Finally alone, I began thinking back to that morning at the Green Lake bed and breakfast. What was that man talking about? It had something to do with the Seattle Monorail, about replacement parts or lack there of. Was there any physical contact between us? Did I shake his hand? No, I remembered he just walked up to where I was sitting and started talking to me. He had a large belly then; a disguise perhaps? He left me saying to have a nice day. That was it. No, wait! As he left he slapped my left shoulder with his right hand. Could he have planted something on me, like a tracking device of some sort? That seemed pretty far-fetched to me, but a possibility.

I decided to check it out. I stood up and walked to the interrogation room door. I stepped into the hallway and was greeted by one of the Gruits standing guard by the door. Evidently I was regarded as a low flight risk. Down the hallway was another Gruit by the bathroom door. I entered the bathroom and shut the door behind me. I walked over to the sink and removed my shirt. Turning around in front of the mirror, I strained to get my head in a position to see the back of my left shoulder. Nothing appeared unusual at first. But the more I focused on my shoulder, a small red dot appeared. It was about the size of a head on a small nail. Its position was right about where the man had slapped my shoulder. I touched it with one of my fingers. The red dot felt sore. Could that guy at the bed and breakfast have placed a tracking device on me that actually dug into and under my flesh? As impossible as that sounded, it would explain how Commander Logan

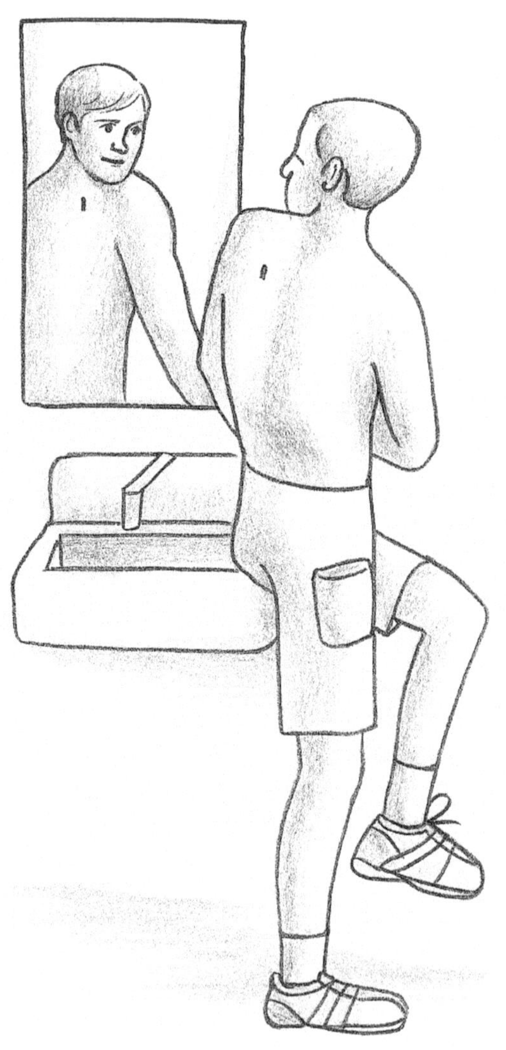

and his Gruits have always known my every move and whereabouts.

Back in the interrogation room I thought about how I could extract the tracking device from my shoulder, if there was one. I wondered if the ETs or Sundance could remove it? It seemed their talents and skills were almost endless. But how could I contact them?

I laid down on the cot. It's been a long, arduous day, I thought. I was tired. Closing my eyes, I fell asleep for a while. I was awakened by the door opening. I slowly looked up. There stood Sundance again. It explained that the electro-magnetic web was no longer a concern. It had been disabled and surveillance was neutralized. We left the interrogation room, boarded its ship and traveled straight to the moon. We entered the crater tunnel that led to the Crystals. Sundance explained that I was to contact the librarian once inside the Crystals. Only the librarian, Sundance said, could help me. What was I going to say to the librarian? Somehow it needed to understand and help me solve the current situation I was in.

Sundance's craft stopped short of the Crystals and I disembarked. Entering a Crystal was always nerve-wracking. It seemed to take the process way too long. Once I finally appeared inside, I called the librarian several times; no answer and no black appeared around me. That's odd, I thought. Usually by now I'd be in black void detention. After a few more tries to communicate with the librarian, I thought maybe Sundance and the other guys could help. I left the Crystal on the slate-gray pathway. I turned around to walk to the ship and abruptly stopped. I was startled, shaken, and horrified at what I saw. Standing in front of me was Commander Logan! Oh, my god! Was this an act of betrayal by Sundance and his crew? "Hello, Mr. McAlister," Logan said with a wry smile on his face.

As if by a sixth sense, I woke up. Geez, thank god that was just a dream! I thought. But something in the room had changed. I looked around and then finally saw the source; the first TV monitor had come on. I stared at the image on the screen. It took just a moment until my worst fears were realized. The image was Kate! They had captured Kate! I had gone from one nightmare to another!

Before I reacted to this horrible situation, I thought about what possible reasons Logan and the Gruits had for holding Kate. Was she now a bargaining chip? I tell Logan what he wants to know and maybe they would let her go? Or, was it for her own safety to be here? I have experienced two attacks while being held by Logan. He had described a third assault. Evidently Logan's Gruits had arrived before any foreign government or terrorist organization could cause Kate harm at home. Either way, she was now a new topic of conversation with Logan.

~Kate,~ I thought. ~If you can hear me, turn your head and look to the right.~ Kate's head turned to the right.

~Mike! I hear you! Are you all right!? Do you know what is going on!?~ Kate asked frantically.

~So far I am fine. What about you? Are they treating you well?~ Mike asked.

~Well, besides being forced to go with these guys in gray suits, they have attended to all my needs. So what is going on!?~ Kate asked.

~It appears our little secret is out; flying to the moon and going back in time. Not only the U.S. government knows, but evidently foreign countries, foreign nationals and perhaps terrorists groups have found out, too. They all want to know how I accomplish these things, I'm sure, for their own purposes. And I think the other reason that Ryan has had us picked up is to protect us,~ I explained.

~Ryan? You call your captor by his first name? And how do you know all these people are after us?~ asked Kate.

Correcting myself, ~Well, Commander Logan and I have a somewhat workable relationship even though I haven't said anything to him yet. I'm assuming that's the other reason you are here, to convince me to be cooperative.~ Mike continued, ~ To answer your other question, since my capture the Gruits and I have been attacked three times by these foreign organizations. I have a huge knot on the left side of my forehead to prove it.~

Kate asked, ~So physically, you're okay?~

~Yes, I am fine. You must be close by for us to communicate like this. Listen, I'm sure Ryan will be stopping by soon since he knows I have seen you on the monitor screen. I need to do some thinking about what questions I need to ask him. After our next interrogation session I will get right back to you.~

~Be careful and be safe. I love you,~ Kate said.

~I love you, too. Talk to you soon.~

Logan entered the command center. Three Gruits were each seated behind computer screens. They all turned towards the door, saw Commander Logan and stood at attention. "Back to work, please," Logan said.

"Rick, status on Mrs. McAlister," Logan asked.

"Mrs. McAlister arrived early this morning. She checked into the barrack's executive suite. She is currently in Interrogation Room 2, sir," Rick reported.

"See to her needs as they arise. Make sure she is comfortable," commanded Logan. Then he added, "Also, turn on the first monitor in Mr. McAlister's room from Interrogation Room 2."

"David, report on Mr. McAlister's failed escape attempt," Logan said.

"The intruder moved with astonishing speed. All surveillance equipment was disabled before we had a chance to respond. Somehow all locks on the elevator and doors were compromised. We monitored Mr. McAlister's movements to the outside of the compound. When it was determined Mr. McAlister was ascending above the base, we quickly engaged the electro-magnetic web. Whatever Mr. McAlister was traveling in failed to penetrate it. He descended back to the base and returned to the interrogation room, sir."

"Did we get any images of the intruder or the supposed aircraft?" Logan asked.

"No, sir. The speed in which the entire operation took place was too fast for us to repair the surveillance equipment in time to monitor the intruder or the aircraft. All surveillance equipment was restored when Mr. McAlister returned to the interrogation room. I might add, sir, whoever it was, their stealth technology is extremely advanced."

Logan thought about what David had said and asked, "Once engaged at full strength, how long does the web stay activated?"

"The web uses an extreme amount of energy. We do not have an adequate energy source for that much output. It will stay activated less than ten minutes each time it is used, sir."

"Thank you David." Logan walked over to the windows overlooking the base. He stared at the distant mountains and thought, I could talk to Mike about the failed escape attempt, perhaps learning something useful. But then he may become aware that we are tracking his every movement. Mike and his cohorts may be leery to try another escape attempt any time soon. Best to leave well enough alone, for now. If there is a next attempt to escape we need to be ready for any eventuality. All personnel, armaments, and aircraft must be standing by prepared to execute the capture of the intruder. And perhaps the sight of his wife being held in an interrogation room may persuade Mike to provide answers about space and time. Then and only then can we move forward to achieve our immediate goals and ultimately, our Mandate.

6

Rosie, Lumpy, Satchmo, and James T exchanged glances. They were extremely uncomfortable. Inside Mr. Wizard they were returning to a place that was, for the most part, forbidden to all of them.

~This is violating the directive of non-interference,~ Lumpy thought. ~Is there another alternative?~

~Our first experience with the directive of non-interference was 1947 at Roswell. We watched one of our crafts and four Observer bodies being taken by the United States government. Craft, craft debris and their bodies were taken from Roswell to Fort Bliss, Texas, then Wright Field in Ohio, and finally, Fort Riley, Kansas. At any one time we could have collected what was left of the craft and our fellow Observers. We could not interfere,~ Rosie thought.

~We now have responsibilities concerning Mike and Kate,~ Rosie continued, ~and the difference between Roswell and now is that we know of extenuating circumstances in this particular situation. If we are to rescue Mike and Kate, then we need to believe these special circumstances warrant our intervention.~

All of the ETs were silent for a very long time. There destination was Homey Airport by Groom Lake, also known as Area 51. It was the home of Base S-4. They knew this intervention had a low probability for success. Everyone needed to be prepared to act accordingly if they had a chance to retrieve Mike and Kate.

"Hey, hold it. Wait a minute. Pump the brakes. This is the author, Larry Alexander, interrupting this Pulitzer Prize for Fiction nominee. Look, I just want to get it all straight, particularly for new readers that have no knowledge concerning these extraterrestrials. And then there are people like me, who actually bought and read the first book, Half Moon, but have memory concerns. Anyway, humor me for a moment.

The ETs call themselves Observers or in their native thought talk

They communicate using a type of telepathy. The ETs habitat is in the moon somewhere. Physically, all ETs are not quite four feet tall. They have large heads with large, black almond-shaped eyes and long slender chins. Their bodies are very thin with two legs and two arms. They have three toes on each foot and three fingers on each hand, plus a thumb of some sort. Extremely dense, the ETs are very heavy and very strong. Their insides are a mystery. Even though on first glance they all look the same, there are subtle differences. The one Mike calls Rosie looks to have a bad case of rosacea around its face. Lumpy has small bumps on its head and Satchmo has a very large forehead, like that of the late Louis Armstrong's, aka Satchmo. James T pilots the craft.

Speaking of their craft, its name is Mr. Wizard; a long story. Google Tooter Turtle and Mr. Wizard. Anyway, the ETs and Mr. Wizard have a symbiotic relationship relying on each other for their existence. Incidentally, Mr. Wizard is a sentient being and out of this universe. It is bio-engineered in another dimension, then brought here in our time and space. This is one reason it can travel ridiculous speeds through our atmosphere utilizing our electro-magnetic-gravitational spectrum. Plus, there is something about buffering time in front of the craft that helps it slice through our gaseous surroundings. I can't explain it, but time is something the ETs just utilize for their own purposes. Sort of like how we humans use water, air, and other natural things for our benefit.

So what are the Observers doing here anyway and how many are there? I can almost answer the latter. There are at least eight. But there could be eight hundred, who knows. And what do they do? What task do they perform? Good questions. The moon is partially hollowed out. Inside are several six-sided green Crystals, some the size of New York skyscrapers. Like a type of religion, the ETs worship these Crystals that were put there by the Creator. I'm not sure who or what the Creator is. You see, the moon is a huge observatory. These Crystals are recording devices. Every person, place, and thing throughout the history of the earth have been recorded in the Crystals. Maybe the ETs supplement the Crystals with specialized information they have gathered on their flights above the earth. For example, UFO's have been sighted at Cape Canaveral during a few of the manned launches. Supposedly UFOs were observed during some of the manned moon missions. Anyway, just think what you could learn about earth's history by gaining access to the inside of these Crystals. Or things you might be able to change.

And that is exactly what Mike can do. In his experiences with the extraterrestrials, he was taught some extraordinary skills. And how did he get involved with the ETs? Well, let's say that after billions of years of observing earth, the ETs were involved in many accidents and crashes. Because of these incidences, Observers were lost. Replacements were needed to carry out their mission. The knowledge of reproduction for the ETs, though, had been forgotten over eons of time. So they selected Mike to help retrieve that information.

Mike's adventures with the ETs began by learning how to meld his mind with that of a humpback whale's mind. This new skill allowed him to enter the Crystal Creation in the moon. Through the Crystals he could travel back in earth's time. To return to the Crystals required Mike to walk through a mist that always surrounded him wherever he was time traveling. Following Mike and his adventures he became lost in his own mind, was thrust into another dimension, and survived a series of natural disasters. However, along the way Mike awakened a sinister dark entity that was obsessed with capturing him. Eventually he came face to face with the dark entity in a black void. After all this, Mike was somehow successful in accessing the reproduction program for the extraterrestrials.

Okay, I'll shut up. Sorry for the interruption, but I hope this background helps. Now you can get back to this intriguing and spellbinding novel."

Commander Logan was seated in the command center studying his notes and reviewing protocols for interrogating hostages, prisoners, and captives. His next interview with Mike had to be fruitful. Alternatives to extracting the needed information was to be avoided.

However, if progress was not achieved he may have no choice in the matter. His superior, the President of the United States, was becoming extremely anxious.

"Commander, sir," David turned in his chair to address Logan. "We have detected a small aircraft traveling at an extremely high velocity. Its elevation is close to the ground evidently not wanting to be detected by radar. For the last several minutes it has not deviated its direction. Their current heading will bring it here, sir."

Looking at David, Logan asked, "At its current velocity, what is the aircraft's ETA?"

"At current speed, eight minutes, sir."

"Please alert the assault team immediately. And emphasize, this is not a drill!" Logan ordered.

With purpose, Logan strode outside the command center and into the sunlight. He made his way to the helicopter pad located next to the command center. Logan approached the four helicopters. They were all Ah-64 Apache Attack helicopters, one of the deadliest gunships in combat. Two crewmen met Logan and helped him into his flight suit. They positioned the stairs to the helicopter's door. Logan climbed into the helicopter's cockpit, positioned himself into the pilot's seat and strapped himself in. As he put his helmet on he thought, I am going to lead three other Ah-64 Apaches in an attempt to capture the approaching aircraft. If successful, this new piece may just complete the puzzle. The helicopter rotors began to turn.

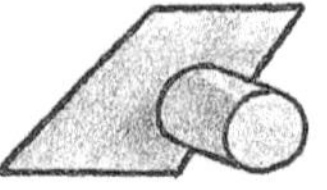

7

Lying on the cot I stared at the white ceiling for quite some time. Except for worrying about Kate and how she must feel about this whole situation, it was tranquil and relaxing. Solitude tends to get a bad rap; it's often equated with loneliness. Really, it's just simply spending time alone that can lead to so many positive things. Sometimes it seems to create a state of peacefulness and can cultivate an overall wellness. Instead of engaging in social media, I thought, people needed to take a break. Get to know and revitalize themselves and see how creative they can become. A friend of mine looks forward to periods of boredom. He says it lets his mind relax and wander while allowing him to create and enjoy new activities; ultimately recharging himself.

Just then the door opened interrupting my thoughts. Lunch had arrived. I got up from the cot and walked over to the table and chairs. I thanked the Gruit for lunch. I sat down while he left and looked at the food; a clear plastic tray containing a ham and cheese sandwich, green salad and French fries. Three small plastic cups containing salad dressing, ketchup, and tartar sauce rounded it out. I spread some of the dressing on my salad with the plastic fork provided. As I ate lunch I wondered when Ryan was going to return. He seemed to be taking longer in between visits. Ryan must know by now that I am aware Kate is being held somewhere in this complex.

I finished eating and began putting all the plastic wrap, plastic silverware, and the little condiment cups back in the plastic tray. As I shoved one of the cups into the others, a thought occurred to me. Somehow, suppose I do have a tracking device planted in me and I had it removed from my shoulder. Where am I going to put it? I guess I could destroy it. On the other hand, perhaps it could be useful in some way. I decided to keep one of the condiment cups with its lid. I wrapped it with part of the napkin and put it in my pocket. I walked to the bathroom with both hands shoved down my pants pockets concealing the cup. I rinsed it and the lid out in the bathroom sink. The guard standing by the interrogation room door gave me a nod as I walked back in and shut the door. The plastic tray on the table was already gone.

Something seemed different. I looked around the room, but didn't see anything new or unusual. I sat down at the table and continued looking. Wait, a second TV monitor was turned on. Now what, I thought? I gazed up at the monitor, but there was nothing visible to see. Then a shape of someone walked by followed by another shape. They looked vaguely familiar. Well, Ryan is going to have to do better then that to break me and give him the information he wants. Still looking at the monitor, it hit me! I quickly stood up and stared closely into the screen. There were Rosie, Satchmo, Lumpy, and James T! They had been captured!

Before I could try to communicate with the ETs, Ryan and a Gruit entered the interrogation room. Walking to the table he said, "Good afternoon Mike. Please sit down." We both sat at the same time.

"I take it Kate has been attended to well," I said in a somewhat condescending voice.

"As you are very much aware, lives are at stake here. We attained your wife yesterday afternoon," Ryan explained. "We were relieved that we arrived at your home before anyone else. And yes, she is being taken care of very well."

I knew Ryan was probably correct in interceding and taking Kate away from possible deadly harm and bringing her here. "Thank you, Ryan. And now you know how I manage to travel to the moon in record time. And I do it naked, too," I said. It appeared Ryan didn't know how to react.

In a few moments, he responded, "I assumed this was your means of lunar transportation." He turned around looking at the second TV monitor. Turning back, he looked at me and said, "What remains is an explanation of your ability to travel back in time?"

"Ryan, tell me how you think you know I went back to 1989 to my home at Ponderosa Estates?" I asked.

Ryan sat very still. Finally, "All right. I will tell you this. Several years ago, even before 1989, we had ways of tracking and monitoring people of interest or people we were directly dealing with. When our team developed an interest in you, one of our associates noticed a strange anomaly when working in our record archives. The computer reported a short twelve minute signal coming from your home in 1989. The explanation is it could only have been you."

"Let's say what you are explaining to me is true, that I did go back to 1989 for twelve minutes. How are you and your team tracking me? What is the device?" I demanded.

"I'm sorry Mike, but that is highly classified information," Ryan said in a matter of fact voice.

"Currently, where are we?" I asked

"That too, is classified," informed Ryan.

"Then I think we are done here, Ryan," I said as I crossed my arms on my chest.

Ryan stared at me for a moment, stood up and walked to the door. As he opened it, he turned to me and said in a threatening manner, "I am disappointed we haven't convinced you that for your sake, for your wife's sake, and for the sake of the extraterrestrial biological entities that you have not cooperated with us. I am afraid that our relationship has now entered a dark and dangerous chapter."

With that ominous threat, Ryan and his companion left.

8

It was a bitter-sweet feeling as we left earth's atmosphere, entered space and headed for the moon. We had escaped from Logan and his Gruits, Base S-4 and Area 51. But, tragically, we had a crewman down. I kept going through every step of our escape plan to figure out what could have gone wrong. Was it preventable? I thought back to when Logan left the interrogation room saying our relationship had entered a new chapter fraught with darkness and danger. Since then I kept thinking about all of the events of this day that had followed his dire warning earlier this afternoon...

~Rosie. Rosie, can you hear me?~ I asked.

~I hear your thoughts Mike. Are you well?~ asked Rosie.

~I am fine, as is Kate. What happened, how did you get captured?~

Rosie didn't exactly answer my questions. ~We are your friends. We are here to assist you and Kate,~ Rosie responded.

~Is Sundance close by?~ I inquired.

~If you are referring to the Observer who did not secure your release from this base, Sundance is close,~ explained Rosie.

~I have an idea on how all of us can get out of here. Please listen to what I am thinking. I seek your opinion if this plan has a chance of succeeding,~ I thought.

Sundance arrived shortly after Rosie and I had developed a plan for escape. ~Greetings,~ Sundance thought as it walked into the interrogation room. ~This room and the surrounding area is secure. Time is important. I do not have the element of surprise. Commander Logan will be better prepared this time.~

~What about the electro-magnetic web?~ I asked.

~The electro-magnetic screen operates for approximately ten minutes before exhausting its power supply,~ explained Sundance.

~Please look here,~ I thought. I pointed to my left shoulder.

~Do I have a tracking device just below my skin, and if so, can you remove it?~

Sundance put its right hand on my left shoulder. Its hand was extremely warm. Immediately, Sundance thought, ~Yes, and yes.~

~Then proceed in extracting it from me, but be careful not to damage it,~ I thought.

During a part of the next minute, I felt excruciating pain like Sundance was digging out the tracking device with some kid's dull pocket knife. ~Geez, Sundance! This process is extremely painful. Is there another method!?~ I was at the point of screaming obscenities. Sundance didn't think anything continuing the painful extraction.

And then, Sundance announced, ~Here is the tracking device.~ He held out his right hand in front of me. It was so small, I didn't see it at first glance. But then there was a glint of silver reflecting from the overhead lights. I finally saw where it was in its hand. It appeared to be metallic and no bigger than the head of a pin.

~How did you get it out of my shoulder?~ I asked Sundance.

~A type of reverse polarity,~ was its answer.

I pulled the small plastic cup out of my pocket and thought, ~Sundance, please put the device in this plastic cup.~

After doing so, Sundance thought, ~We must leave now. Follow me.~ We left the interrogation room. I walked behind Sundance down the hallway past the bathroom. The next door on the right opened and there was Kate and the ETs. They had just joined her. I turned back and looked at Sundance and thought, ~Thank you. See you soon.~

~Yes,~ Sundance responded and left.

I turned towards Kate. We gave each other a big hug and kiss, and I asked, "I am so glad to see you. Are you okay?"

"Yes, I am. And what about you?" asked Kate.

"All things considered, pretty good. So, are the animals being taken care of?"

"Yes. Ronnie said she would watch after them while we were away. So what is happening?" Kate asked.

Turning towards the ETs I confidently said, "We're getting out of here!" ~Guys, it is so good to see you, again. Sorry for the circumstances. Are we on schedule?~

~If Sundance is successful, we will make our way to the surface

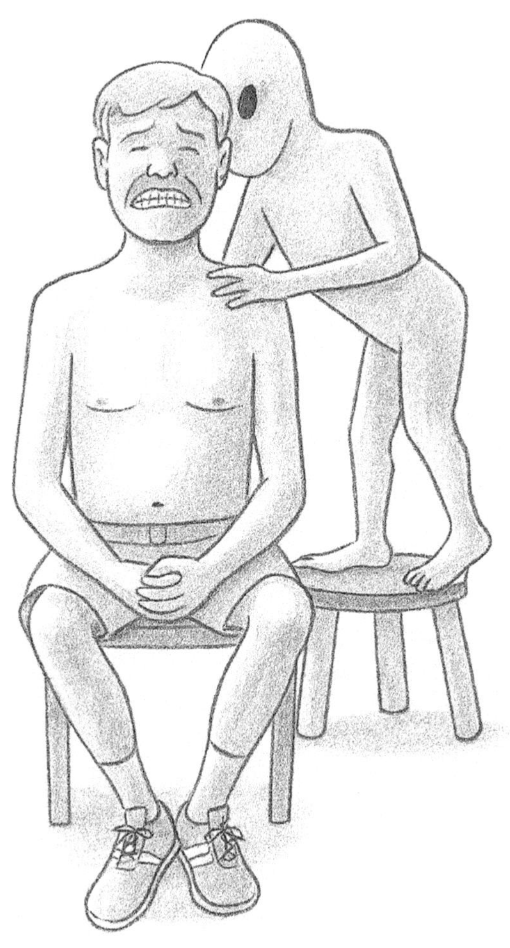

of the base very soon,~ Rosie thought. ~Once outside, we will rendez-vous with our craft. It is being held in a maximum security hangar.~

~Will being in a maximum security hangar be a concern?~ I asked.

~ Being engineered in a different dimension provides our craft with certain advantages,~ Rosie thought.

I smiled and nodded my head.

"Commander Logan, sir. McAlister is on the move. He has entered the elevator. All surveillance and security equipment are currently inoperative," reported David.

Seated at his desk, Logan jerked his head up and turned towards David. How is this possible, he thought? "David, engage the EMS, scramble the aircraft team, and get surveillance and security operatives ASAP! Rick, check on security with the EBE aircraft in the maximum security hangar," ordered the commander.

Logan radioed the aircraft team stressing the importance of nonlethal means of capturing the EBE craft. Steve would lead the team while he commanded operations from the ground. Logan looked at his watch: 15:21. Time was crucial until the EMS would cease functioning.

"Commander, McAlister is airborne. The heading is 337 degrees North Northwest above Base S-4. I will relay that information to the aircraft team, sir," said David.

"Sir," Rick said, "The EBE aircraft is currently secure in the maximum security hangar."

What!? thought Logan. It took him a moment to realize there had to be two EBE aircrafts. "David, have the ground team assemble outside the command center on the double. If the security system continues to be down, I will meet them with search and seizure procedures, "Logan explained.

"Yes, sir!"

Logan moved swiftly to the entrance of the command center. The captured EBEs and McAlister's wife may try to escape using the other aircraft, he thought. We must retrieve them. We cannot lose our current tactical advantage!

The elevator doors opened. Rosie, James T, Lumpy, Kate, I, and Satchmo stepped outside into brilliant sunshine. The temperature was scorching.

~We must move quickly to the maximum security hangar. Follow, please,~ Rosie ordered.

I could see three hangars across the compound about two hundred yards away. Running fast, Rosie led the way with Satchmo bringing up the rear. For dense, heavy things the ETs were surprisingly agile. About halfway I saw one of the hangar side doors opening. Overhead I heard the roar of three attack helicopters presumably trying to bring Sundance, its crew, and his aircraft down. Somehow Sundance had to stall his capture until the EMS ran out of power.

My heart was pounding and it was hard to catch my breath in this heat. Sweat was dripping off of my forehead and into my eyes. Kate was close at my heal. I looked around and gasped, "Are you okay?"

"Don't worry about me. It's just a little bit farther. I'll make it."

Rosie disappeared through the hangar door as did James T and Lumpy. Kate, I, and Satchmo followed. Inside the hangar, I could see Mr. Wizard hovering at the far end. I can't believe it, I thought. Our escape plan just might work.

As we neared, I saw a woman's body in a Gruit uniform on the floor next to the edge of Mr. Wizard. She was not moving. ~Rosie, what happened? Is she all right?~ I asked.

~She will survive,~ Rosie responded.

Rosie entered Mr. Wizard first followed by James T and Lumpy. It then occurred to me that Kate and I had to take our clothes off; no inorganic material allowed inside their ship. I looked at Kate to explain this to her when I noticed what she was wearing.

"I thought this outfit might come in handy," Kate said smiling. These were the same clothes that she had worn traveling to Norway with the ETs; all cotton clothes with leather sandals.

As I stripped, I asked, "Good thinking, but what am I going to do without clothes?" Kate proudly held up her hand holding a leather pouch. When did she bring that, I thought? I didn't even see it.

"I also thought this might come in handy at some point. Hand me your clothes as you take them off."

"You thought of everything," I said.

"Sometimes I can make good decisions, thank you, " she replied.

With my clothes, sneakers, and wallet in the pouch, Kate

entered Mr. Wizard's portal. As she did a Gruit entered the hangar through a side door close to where Mr. Wizard was hovering. "Hey, Carole. I'm here to relieve you," the Gruit said. He looked toward the floating aircraft and saw the disabled woman lying on the floor. As I was going up through the portal and inside the ship I heard the Gruit shout, "Halt, or I will shoot!"

There was a single gunshot. I looked down through the portal and saw Satchmo lying face down on the hangar floor. Immediately I jumped in the portal and was lowered next to Satchmo. First, I looked for the Gruit. I saw him down on his knees and elbows with his hands holding his head. I recognized that pose. The ETs were overloading his brain, not a fun thing to have happen.

~All right Satchmo, here we go.~ I lifted Satchmo up in my arms. Geez, these guys are heavy, I thought. Holding it in with one arm, I lifted my other arm towards the portal and felt being pulled up.

In the meantime, Mr. Wizard disabled the locks of the huge hangar doors. They slowly slid open. ~The EMS is no longer functioning. We may now depart,~ Mr. Wizard thought.

I laid Satchmo face up on the deck of their ship. A clear viscous liquid was oozing from under its back. Satchmo was very still. On my knees, I took Satchmo's right hand in mine. It was extremely warm. I felt a gentle squeeze, then nothing. I looked up and saw Rosie, Lumpy, and James T had formed a semi-circle around Satchmo and me. ~Has Satchmo ceased functioning, Rosie?~ I asked.

~Yes,~ Rosie thought.

Oh no! Satchmo! Satchmo is gone! I put my other hand on top of Satchmo's hand. I felt horrible. I began to cry. Kate came over and put her hand on my shoulder. There were tears streaming down my cheeks. With a faltering voice, I said, "Satchmo saved us. When Kate and I were in my brain with no way out, our friend risked its life and pulled us free. Satchmo saved us!" It was very hard to talk. I was sobbing trying to catch my breath.

I could hear Kate gently crying behind me. I looked up at her. With a quivering bottom lip, I said, "Kate, Satchmo had our back. It stayed behind us making sure that we got safely aboard Mr. Wizard."

With a soft voice, Kate murmured, "I know."

I bowed my head and knelt there for a long time thinking about past experiences with the ETs, particularly Satchmo. I knew we had immediate things to do, but not right now.

After several moments, I slowly rose to my feet, wiped my eyes and hugged Kate. In turn, I gave all of the ETs a hug, too. Each of the ETs carefully lifted Satchmo. They carried it to the aft part of the ship. A hatch door opened and they slowly lowered Satchmo into the compartment below. Silently, the hatch cover closed.

Looking forward in Mr. Wizard I could see the moon approaching, but not as fast as usual. Perhaps it was in respect to our fallen crew member. We traveled in silence. No one thought, no one talked. Thinking back to our escape, there was really nothing that could have been done about the Gruit coming in the hangar to relieve the woman guard. Sometimes it's all just about circumstances, terrible circumstances.

"Mike, are we going home soon, I hope?" Kate asked in a low voice.

I looked at her and said, "Kind of."

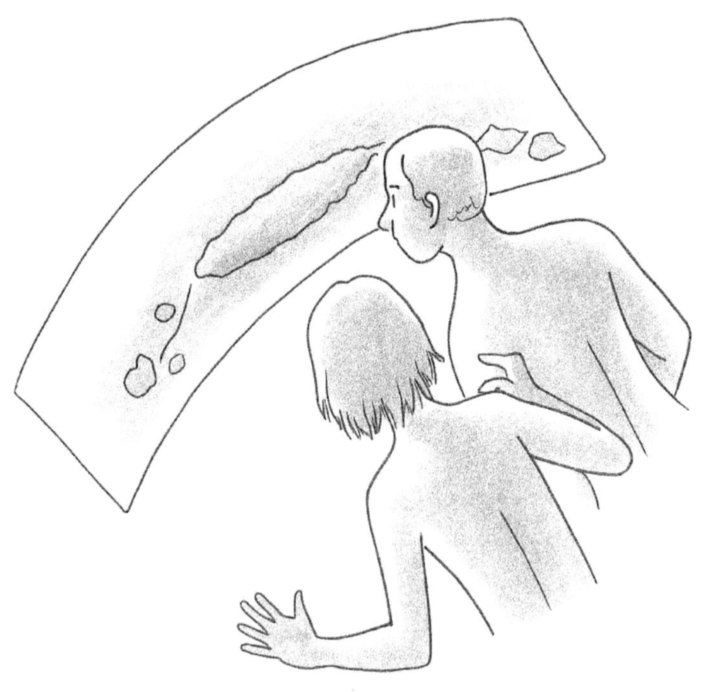

9

"You might want to close your eyes Kate," I advised.

"Why, what's going to happen?" she asked.

I tried to prepare her. "Well, we're going to dive into a crater, travel down a very long tunnel and enter a huge cavern somewhere inside the moon."

"I'll watch," she said confidently.

As the entrance to the crater neared, Kate's grip on my arm became increasingly stronger. "Aren't they going to slow down?"

"They never have before. I think there's some kind of hologram that acts as a camouflage for the tunnel entrance," I explained. We were almost there.

As Kate watched us enter the crater, she yelled, "Oh, my god!" Her hold on my arm became painful as she screamed when we entered the tunnel.

"I tried to warn you," I said, not very sympathetically.

After quite some time of traveling in the tunnel, we entered the cavern. It still looked to me like half the moon had been dug out. It was just huge. I could not see the other side. The ship slowed as we moved towards the green glow far off in the distance.

"Mike, what's that green light?" asked Kate.

"That is our goal. Those are the green Crystals. Believe it or not, those Crystals hold the entire history of the earth from the very beginning. And inside there are crystal plates that contain every event, every thing, and every one that has ever lived on earth," I said. "The Crystals are awesome." We slowly approached them until we came to a stop. The sheer size of the six-sided green Crystals never ceased to be breathtaking.

"They are stunning!" Kate said staring at them in amazement.

"Yes, they are," I answered. "There must be at least fifty of them. Most are as big and as high as New York skyscrapers. I've always wondered how deep they must go into the ground."

Off to the port-side of Mr. Wizard, I saw the other ship. Sundance and its crew were standing by the odd four foot rock wall that surrounded the entire Crystal complex. Rosie and company had already departed our ship and were walking towards them.

"We need to get closer to the Crystals," as I motioned for Kate to enter the portal. Then, I noticed something I had never seen before on the ETs ship. Towards the aft portion were four large boxes. They were approximately four feet long, two feet wide, and about one and a half feet deep. All looked to be constructed of glass and plastic.

"I'll be right there, Kate. I'm going to take a peek at those boxes over there." I walked over and stood by the first one. Looking through the glass, there appeared to be a thick bluish liquid filling the inside of the box. I bent over to see if there was anything else inside. I could make out a faint outline of something floating in the blue fluid. It took some time to identify it. I was stunned when I realized what I was looking at. An ET was staring at me from inside the box! I watched closely. There was no movement from the body. Had it been preserved? If so, for what purpose, I wondered? How weird is that?! I thought I might ask the ETs about this later. But right now, Kate and I had other things to do.

"Anything interesting?" Kate inquired.

"I'll tell you about it later. We need to be getting outside the ship and with the ETs," I said.

"Before I step out, is it safe in the cavern?" Kate asked.

"It's the same medium that is in their ships. You won't experience any discomfort at all," I answered.

Once on the floor of the huge cavern, we walked over to the rock wall and up to Sundance. It held out its hand holding the plastic cup with the tracking device inside. I reached with my hand and took it asking, ~Thank you Sundance. Did you have any problems leaving Base S-4 and arriving here?

~No problems were encountered,~ informed Sundance.

~Good. Please stay in touch from time to time.~

No response.

~Please contact me from time to time,~ I thought.

~Yes. I will contact you at different time intervals,~ responded Sundance. It and its crew walked over to their ship and climbed aboard. The spacecraft turned and slowly flew into darkness.

I looked at Rosie, Lumpy, and James T . ~What will happen to Satchmo?~ I inquired. I couldn't bring myself to say 'Satchmo's body'.

~Satchmo will be taken care of while you are absent,~ explained Lumpy.

Kate looked at me and asked, "What does Lumpy mean 'while you are absent'? Where are we going?"

"You and I have a little journey to take. I hope the results of our travel will be favorable." I stood in front of Kate and held both her hands in mine. With conviction I said, "Trust me." I inserted the plastic cup inside the leather pouch still in Kate's possession. I turned my head towards the guys and thought, ~Thank you all and we will see you soon.~

Hand in hand, Kate and I walked to the nearest Crystal. It leaned a little over the rock wall making it easy for me to touch its side. Kate stared at the Crystal with its shimmering green glow. "Close up, the Crystals are beautiful with how the green color shimmers just beneath the surface," Kate said in amazement.

"Just wait until you see the inside," I commented.

"What!?" Kate shouted alarmingly.

"Okay, hold my hand and don't let go of the leather pouch. Follow my lead as we navigate our way inside please. Here we go. Close your eyes," I instructed.

With my right hand, I touched the Crystals' side. I closed my eyes and found the negative world. With a mental half-twist of my mind, a single slate-gray ribbon appeared leading into the Crystal. It looked something like a wavy sidewalk. ~Kate, do you see the gray ribbon?~ I asked.

~Yes. What do you want me to do?~ she asked cautiously.

~Step on the gray ribbon and follow me,~ I thought. It suddenly became dark, then black. This is the part I didn't like. It just seemed to take a too long to finally get inside the Crystal.

And thinking that, black turned to gray and then changed to a green hue. The diamond-shaped corridor came into focus. It was a geometric wonderland of six-sided shapes on the corridor's walls with no end of the corridor in sight. These hexagonal crystal plates were small; about the size of a playing card. On every crystal plate was an earthly scene: animals, people, nature, events, and buildings.

~Mike, this is astounding! And every living thing has their own crystal plate?~ Kate asked as she looked all around her.

~Every living and non-living thing. Listen, I must hurry,~ I stressed. ~I don't want to stir up the librarian. He is not a part of this plan, yet.~

As we stood in the corridor, I put my hand next to a crystal plate. With my mind, I found the place and time that we needed to visit. ~All right Kate, don't let go.~ Kate tightened her grip on my left hand.

Hot, with the scent of ponderosa pine trees and a hint of sage brush. Kate and I had materialized at Ponderosa Estates and the site of our old home. I started to get dressed behind the barn's lean-to that protected bailed hay and next year's firewood. I scanned the ground surrounding us to make sure there weren't any rattlesnakes crawling around.

I looked at Kate and saw her incredulous expression as she viewed our old barn. "Mike, what in hell are we doing here?" She sounded upset. Just then Babe, Kate's quarter horse mare, meandered around the end of the barn evidently hearing a familiar voice.

"Babe?! Mike, what are you doing to me?" It really wasn't a question. As Babe came up to Kate, she reached out petting and stroking Babe's neck. Babe nickered several times.

"Look, I didn't think you would come if I told you where we were going. I really didn't have time to explain. But I just didn't see any other alternative. And the ETs agreed. Come on. Let's go see what we're up to," I said, trying to inject a little humor. It appeared that it didn't work or help the situation.

As we walked around the front of the barn, we stopped and looked north towards the town of Tonasket. The log home sat perched on a small hill and in its own way had a stunning view. There were low lying green pastures of alfalfa checkered with brown fields that had been recently harvested, acres of sagebrush in between the fields, and rounded mountains in the distance. It was a beautiful day with plenty of blue sky and some cirrus clouds lending texture to the atmosphere.

We slowly strolled to the log home not really knowing what to expect from us. Would we be accepted or told to vanish the way we came, through the thick haze that is just a ways around the house and the barn? Just then, the back door of the log home opened and my younger self stepped out onto the back porch that faced the barn. He came down the steps and appeared to be heading in our direction. Well, here we go, I thought.

We stopped in the driveway and looked towards young Mike. Eventually he lifted his head in mid-stride, saw us and stopped. We stood staring at each other for an uncomfortably long time; he with his youthful looks and longish auburn hair and me at sixty years old with wrinkles and shortish gray hair. He then lifted his left arm appearing to look at a watch. I've never ever worn a watch. It was just as I would have done myself.

"Is that thirty-five years up already?" he asked us sarcastically. We walked towards each other simultaneously lifting our right arms and shook hands. I always wondered what my shake grip was like; pretty good.

"Who did you bring with you?" he asked, looking at Kate.

"Your wife," I said.

He squinted his eyes as he tilted his head a touch looking at Kate. He took a step forward and gave Kate a hug. "Welcome back to 1989 Kate." Then young Mike turned to me and asked, "What are you doing here... again?"

"We need your help," I said.

He stood for a moment and finally asked, "Is it still MacNaughton and Seven Up? And Kate, chardonnay?"

Kate said, "Yes, a chardonnay would be great," while I said, "It's now MacNaughton and Coke Zero."

He turned towards the log home, took a couple steps and then spun back around to us. "Coke what?"

Being agreeable, I said, "Mac and Seven will be just fine."

"I'll meet you on the front porch with the drinks," he informed us as he went into the house.

On the front porch were four old wooden chairs with blue pillow cushions on each. Dividing the four chairs was a small wooden table. I didn't remember where they had come from, but it fit the log home western motif. Kate and I both sat down enjoying the view to the north. Out of the left corner of my eye, I saw movement. Looking that way here came NIckie with her tongue hanging out, panting. She climbed the porch steps towards Kate and me. I let out a big sigh; Nickie, our family dog.

She was an English springer spaniel with liver saddleback colorings. "Nickie," I called. She came right up to me and as before, lowered her head to be petted. I stroked her head and neck and then scratched the back of both ears. I started to mist up; way too emotional for me. Just then young Mike came out of the front screen door with the drinks. I looked up at him with tears in my eyes. Nickie then walked over and put her head on Kate's lap.

"I see you and Nickie are getting reacquainted." He put my drink on the armrest of the chair and handed Kate her glass of chardonnay. Kate and I both said thank you. I took a sip, perfect. Even in my youth I mixed a fairly strong drink.

"Where are the boys?" I asked. If they were here I didn't want them getting freaked out seeing so many parents.

"Trav is working at Hal's IGA today and Joel is at little league basketball practice." Young Mike sat down and continued, "So, what is it I can do for the both of you?"

Before I could respond young Kate came out the screen door. I looked up to see long blonde hair. I didn't remember Kate having such blonde color to her hair. She looked at us with a dumbfounded expression. "Oh....hello." Then she looked at young Mike. "I wondered why you had three drinks. Where's mine? I have a feeling I'm going to need at least one. What is this all about?"

"It seems the future isn't as bright as it should be," young Mike exclaimed.

"Well, I guess introductions really aren't needed. As we told Mike when we first arrived we need his and your help," I explained. Mike got up and went into the house.

"What happened to 'this will all make sense in about thirty-five years'?" young Kate asked accusatorily.

"When Mike returns I will do my best to answer your question," I said. An awkward couple of moments later, Mike returned with another chardonnay for young Kate. He may need a couple of bottles before this whole thing is over, I thought.

"Okay. Please listen," I said calmly. "Kate and I are here from several years in the future, so in that context what I am going to say shouldn't be too alarming. But I am going to try and explain how we got to our current situation without giving away too much about the future. And then I'll explain how you can help us." I began:

Early one morning Kate and I were awakened by a strange pulsating green light coming from outside our house. I went to investigate and saw four extraterrestrials on our yard with their ship hovering above them. When I went outside and asked them what they were doing, they explained that they were refueling their flying saucer with old and sick deer.

Young Kate interrupted, "To me this seems way stranger than you traveling through time to 1989".

"Okay," I said with a smile. "Just wait." I continued:

As the ETs were boarding their ship, I asked if I could go on a joy ride with them. They said to reach up into the portal under the ship. They took me to Seattle and Mars that morning. I was home before Kate woke up. So for some reason the extraterrestrials chose me to help them with a specific concern of theirs. After millions, perhaps billions of years they had forgotten how to reproduce. I was to help them by finding the answers to their reproduction process.

"Excuse me," said young Kate interjecting again. "Why you?"

Remembering what the ETs had told me, I answered, "They found me 'surprisingly reasonable and patient.'" Looking at young Kate I asked, "What do you think?" She just rolled her eyes a touch. I carried on with my story.

As it turns out the moon is a huge receptacle for earth's history, like a satellite dish. It gathers all information from earth and stores that information in huge green Crystals. These Crystals are located some-where inside the moon in a huge, vast cavern. The ETs were convinced the reproduction answer was inside those Crystals. They are not al-lowed to enter the Crystals. It's like some kind of religious monument to them. But I could, so they taught me how to get inside. There was only one problem. Something was already residing in the Crystals and it didn't like me at all. It called itself the librarian. Evidently it was in charge of the information gathering, categorizing, and storage. I real-ly don't know what it did.
Anyway, it and I had a short conversation. I told it I was there on be-

half of the ETs searching for the answers to their reproduction process. It said I went to a lot of trouble for nothing because the information I was after did not exist in the Crystals. And then it kicked me out. But, the answer was in the librarian. Before I left the Crystals, it evidently planted that information in my mind. When I returned to the ETs waiting outside the Crystals, they immediately read what the librarian had implanted in me and were ecstatic. I had the reproduction information they needed.

Interrupting my story, young Mike asked, "None of that explains why you are here. What help do you need from us?"

"Good point Mike. So far that is just half the story," I said and continued on:

Everything was fine with Kate, me, and the ETs. We hardly saw much of them, only occasionally. Then somehow the word got out that I could go to the moon in three minutes and travel back in time. A strange military organization, I suspect, buried deep in the United States government found out about my amazing abilities. Their superior officer, Commander Ryan Logan, had a tracking device planted in me. It was buried in my shoulder when I came here earlier to get some of my clothes. Somehow a computer picked up the blip from old 1989 surveillance records.
Because of all this, Kate and I have both been captured and held hostage by this military outfit that calls themselves Gruits. However, ETs have extraordinary abilities. Having disabled the Gruits surveillance system, an ET came to my interrogation room and extracted the tracking device from my shoulder, which hurt like hell by the way. It is now in a plastic cup here in Kate's leather pouch. Another ET ship and crew pretended to be captured by Commander Logan and the Gruits. So, the first ship took the tracking device and kept the Gruits busy chasing them. Kate, I, and the other ETs escaped in another ship undetected. So by now Ryan, Commander Logan that is, must know that Kate and I have escaped to the past because the tracking device is going to show another blip now from their 1989 records. There, end of the story.

Looking at both young Kate and Mike I said, "All right, so the favor we are asking is this; can Kate and the device stay here for a while? Logan will continue thinking we, particularly me, are both staying here in 1989. This will allow me to be unencumbered when going ahead in time and looking for a solution to our problem. In other words, Ryan cannot track me anymore in my present time."

Young Mike looked at young Kate. "I don't think we have a choice. We have to help them. Kate?" asked young Mike.

Looking at me, young Kate asked, "Do you ever remember meeting your older self here? And if you don't, how can you be so sure Mike and I will be safe?"

I never thought about that one before. Trying to explain I said, "Look, as far as I know I am the only earthling that has access to the Crystals, let alone the ability to pick a time and place in the past to visit."

After a few moments, young Kate said convincingly, "Of course Kate can stay with us as well as the device."

I looked at Kate and thought, ~Does this sound okay to you?~

Nodding her head, she thought, ~I don't see any other way. It looks like you and the ETs had a thorough plan. So what is happening from here on out?~

Addressing young Kate and Mike, I said, "Kate just asked me what exactly the plan is for us to go back to our time and lead normal lives."

"I didn't here her say anything," young Mike said, somewhat confused.

"Sorry, you're right. When you're around the ETs long enough, you can acquire the ability to think thoughts like mental pictures or snapshots that others can read and understand. I call it thought talk. Anyway, first, we accept your offer. Thank you so much. And as for the plan, I will return to the Crystals and confront the librarian. I will describe our situation and hopefully, it can come up with an acceptable solution for us," I explained.

"And if it doesn't?" young Mike asked.

"Well, I always thought the loft in the barn here would make a great guest apartment," I said kiddingly.

Young Kate stood up, looked at Kate and said, "Come on. I know your dying to see Babe."

Kate finished her wine, got out of the chair and said thanks to young Mike. The two Kates left for the barn. I looked at young Mike, held up my empty glass and asked, "One more before I go?"

When he returned with another drink, I was staring at the outside of the dining room. It was just off the front porch. "Hey, do you remember the time when the in-laws were staying here and we served spaghetti for dinner that night?" I asked.

"You mean when Jack mistook a bowl of Thousand Island dressing for spaghetti sauce and loaded a bunch of it on his spaghetti noodles?" young Mike asked.

"Yeah," I said with a big smile on my face. "And once Kate brought over and set down the real sauce on the dining table did he finally figure out he had put salad dressing on his noodles."

And young Mike finished the story. "I watched Jack try to cover up his mistake. He folded his noodles over on top of the dressing and then put on the real spaghetti sauce. Amazingly, he ate the whole thing anyway."

We started laughing and could hardly stop. There were other stories we could share, but I needed to go and try to solve this dilemma Kate and I were in. Maybe another time for reminiscing.

I finished my drink, got out of the chair and said, "Mike, thank you again. I will try to return to get Kate as soon as I can." We shook hands.

"I know you will and you're welcome. Good luck," young Mike said sincerely. "Wait a minute." He went in the house and returned with a couple bottles of water and handed them to me. "You may need these," he said. "Oh, and maybe you can do me a favor. Bring me back something from the future."

Before I left, I told Kate to be sure and not walk into the mist that was surrounding the house and barn. Otherwise, she would be back in the Crystals with no way out and in the company of the librarian.

With tears in our eyes, we hugged and kissed. Kate handed me the leather pouch. "Here is the pouch. Please come back soon. I love you!" Kate said affectionately.

"I will. I promise." I said. "I love you, too." I turned and walked into the mist and vanished.

10

Commander Logan was furious. Not on the outside, of course. He had to exhibit calm and confidence. But inside he was seething. He had overestimated his team's abilities and underestimated the extraterrestrial's abilities. And certainly McCalister's. I will never, ever make that critical mistake again, he thought. We were so close to reaching our primary objective of the Gruits' Mandate.

It appeared to be business as usual in the command center except Logan, Rick, and Scott were packing up computers, supplies, and personal belongings. There were other fish to fry at other locales. Only David was engaged with his computer.

"Commander, sir. It has been reported to me that a signal has just shown up on our surveillance records from 1989. It appears that after McAlister's escape, he has returned to the past."

Interesting, thought Logan. Hmmm. I still believe McAlister will return to us. Once he thinks everything through, who else is going to protect him? Maintaining composure Logan said, "Thank you David for the update. When we arrive at Joint Base Andrews please provide a detailed briefing to me concerning McAlister's latest travels and current whereabouts." When briefed about McAlister, Logan was scheduled to meet with the President about any progress with McAlister and his unique talents. With this president, Logan thought, failure was never an option.

Humanity. In a corridor of one of the green Crystals, I was surrounded by humanity being displayed on millions of small crystal plates appearing like a honeycomb on the walls. Sympathy, compassion, and generous behavior were the common bonds. I wondered how we were doing in that regard. Are our attributes beginning to weaken towards one another? Are crimes against humanity multiplying? Perhaps treating all creatures with kindness, tenderness, and respect are fading values. I am hoping though, that humanity is not just an earthling attribute, but that the librarian will exhibit some of these human qualities, too.

The crystal corridor began to darken when suddenly I was whisked away in a wind gust of blackness. Still conscious I found myself floating in the black void. Once again there was no ceiling, no walls and no floor. A place where gravity and light doesn't exist. I wondered if this black void was present somewhere in the moon or was it a device strictly created and utilized by the librarian?

Suddenly, I felt sick to my stomach, a sure sign the librarian was here. In a booming voice,

"WHY HAVE YOU RETURNED!?"

Startled, I tried to gather my composure. "I have come back seeking your assistance," I said calmly.

No response.

Thoughtfully, I said, "You know, it would help if I could see who I am addressing."

"The black void, as you refer to it, is my habitat."

"Can you see me in this blackness?" I asked.

"Yes. I do not need light to assist my visual senses. My sight comes from bodily sensors," it responded.

"I feel your ability to see me and the fact that I cannot see you gives you an unfair advantage with any conversation we engage in." I was becoming increasingly tired of its superior attitude towards me.

"I am not negotiating with a sentient species who is barely able to converse at all in evolutionary terms about the proprieties of conversation!" raged the librarian.

That was it. My patience with a life form that probably has been in existence for billions of years was over. Speaking calmly and with confidence I challenged the librarian by saying, "Perhaps this will help you 'see the light'. Do you have any defenses that will protect the Crystals from outside interference or attack?"

Silence.

"I thought so," I said. Continuing, "An intelligence organization deep within the United States government has discovered that I possess special abilities that the Observers have taught me. Sooner or later, either through bribery, coercion, or chemicals I will be forced to divulge the existence of the Crystals in the moon. Just think of the possibilities if access to the Crystals was possible by the United States or any other country or organization. The potential use of the Crystals is almost endless; going back in time and altering events to gain advantage or fortune in the present. The power to an individual or organization would be staggering!"

The blackness began disappearing. I held up my hand in front of my face and could see all of my fingers. I pulled my hand down and then I saw it! My initial reflex was to get away from whatever it was. I started kicking my legs and waving my arms and hands furiously, like I was swimming to avoid a predator. But there was no substance to the space around me. Kick and wave all I wanted, I wasn't going anywhere.

About four feet in front of me was this...thing. No bigger than a kitchen toaster, it was somewhat oval-shaped like a football, and all black. The black part appeared to be slowly bubbling almost all over its bodily surface. A bubble would grow then recede. The growth of the bubbles seemed to be independent from one another. And there was a hissing sound each time a bubble would appear. Not all of the bubbling black ball was visible. There was a grayish gas resembling storm clouds, covering about fifty percent of the shape.

The last feature I saw were octopus-like arms. No longer than a foot or so in length, they would slowly grow outwards while moving in different directions. They reminded me of a snake's tongue, darting out and quivering up and down. Then they would disappear back into the oval shape. Sometimes there were three arms, other times five. And the smell it produced was a very strong vinegar smell, like acetic acid. It was the most hideous thing I had ever seen or smelled in my life!

"What assistance are you seeking from me?"

Oh my god!! This was the librarian!? The sudden urge to throw up was overwhelming. I was having a horrible time trying to regain any semblance of composure.

"P...p...please g...give me a mo...ment." I was having trouble speaking. I took three deep breaths, closed my eyes and began slowly counting to ten. Maybe I should keep my eyes closed, I thought. No, I asked to see it. Now I have to look at it.

I opened my eyes and stared at the librarian. I slowly began explaining the events of the last two days involving Kate and me. All the while the librarian hissed, steamed, bubbled, and smelled. I began

to wonder if I was wasting my time with the librarian. Could it actually do anything to help Kate and me return to normal lives? I had high hopes that somehow the librarian would wave a magic wand of some sort and fulfill my request. But I was beginning to feel the anguish of defeat.

I finished my story ending with our escape from the Gruits and leaving Kate safely in the past with the tracking device. Concerned, I said, "So librarian, I am requesting your help. Can you return Kate and me back to leading normal lives with no interference from anything or anybody?"

I was completely surprised when the librarian, without hesitation answered, "I will fulfill your request. However, there are two conditions that you will have to meet. The first is time management. Return here in three earth days with your mate," ordered the librarian. Then there was a pause, as if it was searching for the right words to explain the second condition.

"Yes, we can comply with the first condition and return here in three days," I answered. "And what is the second?"

"Your memory of the Crystals, of me and the Observers will be extracted from your minds!" declared the librarian.

After Mike had left involuntarily, the librarian had grown exhausted. It was rigorous maintaining such a small size in the surrounding light. ~It was necessary not to alarm the human being. I did not want the earthling to see my actual size. He may have panicked and tried to escape. His earthly concerns are now truly my concerns, too. But I must return to my normal size,~ the librarian thought. For it, normal size was as large as a Blue Bird school bus. The librarian needed at least three earth days just to regenerate from its experience of maintaining a miniature size with the earthling. And then it thought, ~I should have consumed the earthling the first time we had met.~

11

I had slept twelve hours. At least that's what the ETs told me. I don't even know where I slept. I awoke standing up. It was certainly needed. Except for catnaps in the interrogation room, I couldn't remember the last time I had a decent sleep. Anyway, I found myself in Mr. Wizard with the ETs flying somewhere above earth. I noticed the leather pouch was still around my shoulder.

I cannot get the image of the librarian out of my mind. That was the most hideous creature I had ever come in contact with. I now know why it prefers existing in a totally black environment. However I feel about it, the librarian is our only hope of fixing the terrible situation that Kate and I find ourselves in. Except I am truly disappointed in what the results of this solution entails. Our memories of the ETs will be wiped from our minds forever; our friendships and all of our experiences together will be gone.

When I shared this with the ETs they were genuinely upset. I thought, ~Guys, is there any other answer to the situation that Kate and I are in? It seems to me with all the resources at your disposal there has to be another way.~ Rosie, Lumpy, and James T kept looking at one another. I couldn't understand what they were communicating. All I know is if there wasn't an alternative solution, I had to go back in three days and visit the librarian again; this time with Kate.

~Mike,~ Rosie thought. ~The three of us have reached a consensus that there is something you need to witness. We are going to take you to it now. But for this to happen, travel to the fourth planet is necessary. Are you in agreement?~

~The fourth planet,~ I thought. ~You mean Mars? What is on Mars that I need to see?~

~You must see and experience what we are going to show you firsthand,~ Rosie thought. ~We cannot reveal what it is for fear you would form preconceived ideas or thoughts before we arrived at Mars.~

71

I did not know what they were up to, but I didn't think I had a choice. Maybe it would help with a different solution. ~I am in agreement as long as it doesn't interfere with meeting the librarian in three days,~ I thought firmly. I could feel that there was something they were holding back. Oh well, I've no where to go for awhile. I might as well see what they had to show me. Besides, I really did enjoy astronomy and planetary study. When I was pursuing my fifth-year to fulfill my education degree years ago I needed a five credit class, any class. So I signed up for Astronomy 101. Since they were easy credits to attain it was football, basketball players and me in attendance each day. It turned out to be the best college class that I had ever taken.

Immediately Mr. Wizard stopped and shot straight up into the blue sky. As blue turned to black I began feeling a tingling sensation throughout my body, like a bad case of goose bumps. The last time this happened Rosie explained to me that as we approach and come close to the speed of light, this sensation would dissipate. Rosie stated that their top speed was 250,000 kilometers per second. It should be a short trip to Mars.

I looked to the back of the ship. The boxes were gone. ~Rosie, when we were in the moon I noticed four plastic and glass boxes towards the aft of Mr. Wizard. I had never seen them before. I looked in one and saw an Observer,~ I thought, concerned.

Rosie and Lumpy turned and stared at me for a moment. Finally, Lumpy thought, ~The contents were fellow Observers. They were lost in New Mexico in 1947, your time. Those boxes had been stored at Base S-4 for many years. We took the opportunity to retrieve the deceased Observers and return them to our lunar habitat.~

I stood looking at the ETs and eventually thought, ~I am sorry about your fellow Observers. I am glad you brought them back where they belong. If you don't mind my asking, why did it take you so long to acquire them?~

~Observers are never to interfere with earthlings. We believe Commander Logan has changed certain conditions, one being your capture and his subsequent knowledge of your lunar travels. And, there is more.~ Rosie continued, ~After the commander thought he had captured us, we took advantage of these changing conditions and attained the lost Observers.~

Before I could ask Rosie what 'the more' was, James T announced that we would soon be orbiting Mars.

Mars! There it was right before us. Stark, lifeless, cold, but deceptively beautiful. Brush strokes of orange, red, and brown colors were accented by vast plains in the north and meteor craters lending texture to the south. The planet was astounding and humbling. From early telescopes showing the appearance of a water canal network on Mars' surface to H.G. Wells *War of the Worlds*, and now recent speculation about spacecraft images showing pyramids and the 'Face on Mars', man has always been fascinated with the planet. Planetary astronomer, Carl Sagan, wrote in his book *Cosmos* that 'Mars is a kind of mythic arena onto which we have projected our Earthly hopes and fears.'

As I gazed at the red planet Mr. Wizard had stopped descending. It appeared we were in a stationary orbit above Mars. I wondered what I should be observing thousands of miles above Mars' surface. ~Rosie,~ I thought, ~What am I supposed to be looking at?~ Rosie walked to the port side of Mr. Wizard. I followed it and was astounded at what was just outside the ship! We were orbiting Mars next to Phobos, one of Mars' moons.

There was no mistaking Phobos. Its unique features included a surface pockmarked with craters, the moon's remarkably dull gray color and Phobos' shape that wasn't quite round. And there was Stickney Crater, about six miles in diameter dominating Phobos' surface. Phobos, son of the Greek god of war, Ares. However, Mars was named for the Roman god of war. Phobos - phobia - fear. I suddenly experienced a chill going down my spine. Why were we here?

~You must be careful. Solar winds can electrically charge the shaded side of the moon,~ Rosie explained. ~It would be like experiencing a static shock, certainly not life threatening but surprising. Also, examine the many unusual grooves on Phobos' surface. These are stress marks caused by Mars' gravity. There could be tremblers or small quakes.~

~Rosie, why are you thinking all of this?~ I asked, somewhat concerned.

~We will be traveling inside Phobos,~ Rosie thought.

~Okay, as long as I've got company~, I responded.

A somewhat different entrance than going into the moon, we slowly approached and went into a small crater. Similar to the moon's crater entrance we appeared to go through a type of hologram representing the crater's floor. Eerily similar to the inside of the moon's massive cavern, this one also looked as if it had been purposely carved out. This cavern's surroundings were lit with the same pale green light. We turned a corner and...you've got to be kidding me... there in front of us were large green crystals; not as big as the moon's Crystals, not as many, and not as bright. But there they were.

As we approached, I had so many questions that I wanted answers to. Is Mars being observed in the same way that earth is? Are there Observers here? Is a librarian involved? If so, where are the Martians or other forms of life? Or did they go somewhere? If there weren't any Martians, was a librarian just observing the surface of Mars watching bands of clouds, dust devils, and carbon dioxide freezing? My mind was racing!

~Guys, is this the same type of operation that is currently taking place in the earth's moon?~ I asked.

Rosie turned and looked at me and thought, ~It is similar. It is different~.

What does that mean, it is similar and it is different? Is this like a puzzle or mystery that Rosie wants me to figure out?

~You must go inside the Phobos crystals. You must see for yourself what is similar and what is different.~ It was like Rosie and the guys were challenging me. I have had enough experience with them to know that they weren't going to supply any answers. I had to find the answers myself. And that meant entering Phobos' crystals.

Mr. Wizard stopped an appropriate distance from the crystals. I walked to the portal. I still had the leather pouch strapped around my neck and hanging under my left arm. As I was lowered to the inside surface of Phobos, I heard Rosie think, ~We will await your return.~

When my feet made contact with the sandy floor, dust wafted up all around me. It gave the appearance that this cavern and these crystals had been around for a long, long time. I looked ahead and found something similar; a four foot rock wall circumventing the crystals. I took one step and literally flew like a projectile over the rock wall and headed directly to the first large crystal. I had forgotten that there was very little gravity on or in Phobos. I struck the crystal head on. I tried lessening the blow with my hands and arms. Like a carom, I

bounced off and hit the neighboring crystal with my backside. I tried
to slow my movement by sliding my hands across the crystal's sides.
Somewhat successful, I still couldn't stop long enough to put my hand
securely on a crystal's surface so I could enter inside.

I looked around for an answer. To my right were two crystals
extremely close together; just maybe that might work, I thought.
Pushing off the crystal I was next to, I slowly floated to the two crystals. Wedging myself between them, I finally came to a stop. All right
I said to myself, I think I can stay here long enough to get inside. I
reached out in front of me and carefully laid my hand on one of the
crystal's six sides. Closing my eyes, I found the negative space, and
with a half-twist of my mind, a gray slate ribbon appeared, waving
its way from the crystal to me. I stepped onboard the ribbon and
was pulled inside the crystal and into blackness. As with the moon's
Crystals, it took a concernedly long time before my surroundings were
bathed in a pale green light. Eventually, I found myself inside a diamond-shaped crystal corridor stretching out ahead of me with no apparent end in sight. And each wall of the corridor contained millions
of small crystal hexagonal plates. I wondered if there was a librarian
taking care of these, just like in the moon?

Randomly, I picked one of the hexagonal crystal plates to look
in. It was blank; no image, just a blank plate. I looked at other hexagonal plates near me and they were all blank, too. Looking above and in
back of me, every plate was blank. That was really odd. I'd never seen
a blank hexagonal plate in the moon's Crystals. Just then, the corridor
wall began moving towards me. It collided with my right shoulder
throwing me across the corridor hitting the wall behind me. The corridor movement finally came to a stop. Was that one of those quakes or
tremblers Rosie had warned me about? The leather pouch strap had
become tangled around my arm. I untangled it, but in this near zero
gravity the pouch and strap had become a nuisance. I should have
left it back in the ship, I thought.

Is this what the ETs wanted me to see? If so, I didn't understand what it all meant. As I stood looking at blank hexagonal plates, it
occurred to me that maybe all the plates had stopped recording any
and all activities on the Martian surface at the same time. To make
time go backwards in the moon's Crystals, I would have to push on the
left side of the hexagonal plate. I didn't hesitate. I picked a plate and

began pushing on its left side. Nothing was happening. I kept up the pressure. Suddenly, the plate lit up! I looked inside. It was a Martian landscape. There was nothing really discernible or interesting, just sand, rocks, and stone rubble. Maybe I should go back in time a little more. I pushed the left side again for several seconds. When I stopped and looked in the plate, I was in total amazement.

There was a community of circular buildings with dome-shaped roofs. Some were wide, some not. One-story buildings and others with two-stories were a part of the countryside. Brownish-red in color, they probably used local materials. There didn't seem to be any roads, just trails in the sand that linked most of the buildings. I quickly counted about twenty structures. Off to the left was a massive rectangular building. Its roof was also domed, but in a different construction style. It was a hipped roof, but the sides and ends were rounded.

Vegetation appeared to be sparse, resembling that of arid and semi-arid regions on earth. Unexpectedly, the crystal corridor's walls began shaking. After a few moments they dramatically started waving in and out. Once again, the leather pouch strap got tangled, this time around my right arm restricting its movement. I grabbed the strap with my left hand and gave a big tug. My right arm became free, but I couldn't control the reaction this had on my body. I flew towards the corridor wall and onto the hexagonal plate depicting the Martian community. With my fingers pushing on the side of the plate, I avoided touching it. Heaving a sigh of relief, I then watched in horror as the leather pouch bounced onto the crystal plate's surface. Suddenly, I was no longer in the crystal corridor.

12

Keeran woke up early. She was excited, probably more like nervous anticipation. There was going to be another qualitative analysis lab in chemistry today, her favorite class. To think, she thought, that there are only 118 known elements that make up the entire universe just astounded her. The fascinating thing to Keeran was the study of atoms and molecules that formed chemical compounds and molecular bonds. She could spend hours writing molecular formulas from different types of compounds.

Anyway, there had been a series of qualitative analysis labs at school this year. Participating in these labs gave students an opportunity to earn points in a global competition. The eventual winner would be crowned Student Chemist of the Year, the highest honor a chemistry student could achieve.

Three labs were left before the school year ended. Keeran was currently tied for first place. A first place finish today and she would be that much closer to the regional competitions. Keeran knew no mistakes could be made today during the qualitative analysis lab.

Keeran finished getting dressed, gathered her school supplies and headed out the door. "Goodbye mom," she called. Keeran knew dad was already at work.

"Keeran, what's the rush? You haven't had breakfast yet," her mom said concerned.

"I have a lab today and wanted to get an early start," Keeran explained.

Keeran's mother knew how important these labs were to her and decided not to press the issue. She simply said, "Good luck, dear!"

"Thanks," and out the door Keeran went.

Normally Keeran would meet up with a couple of her friends and walk to school together talking about school activities, parents, school gossip, but mainly about boys. Keeran had decided she wanted to walk alone this morning so she could concentrate on reviewing potential compounds that might be used in the lab; their chemical and common names. Her friends would understand.

Chemistry was first period. After entering the school, Keeran made her way down the hall, into the commons area and finally through the chemistry classroom's door. She sat at her usual desk and began reviewing the notes she had taken this past week. Sodium and calcium were two of the elements that the students had studied. Lost in thought, she heard someone from behind address her. Keeran looked up to see Trace, the young man she was tied with for first place lab points. "Oh, hi Trace. Sorry, I was doing some last minute studying for the lab. How are you?" Keeran asked.

"I'm good," Trace said. "Are you ready for the big lab this morning?"

"Oh, I'm never quite ready, but I'm really looking forward to it. And you?"

"Exactly the same. I hope you do well," Trace said as he went to his desk.

"You, too!" Keeran called after. Trace was a nice, considerate guy, she thought.

Classroom lights flashed as Mr. Rissin entered the classroom. He was young, attractive, popular amongst the students, and quite the showman as he would use the front of his classroom as if it was a theater stage. You could tell that he loved teaching.

Standing by his lab station and desk he heartily exclaimed, "Good morning everyone! As you are aware this is the eighth qualitative analysis lab in a series of ten. The person with the most earned points after the tenth lab will move on to regionals. And looking at the standings, everyone of you in this class has the opportunity to become the lab point leader after today."

Pushing a small four-wheel cart, Mr. Rissin went to each of the ten student lab stations delivering the unidentified compounds, all the while discussing today's lab. "You will attempt to identify eight compounds. This morning I have included the testing agents that you will need. In this lab, a flow chart is not required. Simply list each compound's chemical name, formula, and common name corresponding to the number on the test tube. For your enjoyment, I have added a couple of surprises. You will have thirty minutes to complete the qualitative analysis lab. Let me remind you that the person completing the lab before anyone else will receive two extra points. However, accuracy is of the utmost importance. Any mistakes in your answers will erase those two points. Any broken equipment will also result in a deduction of points. Come to me for replacements if that occurs."

"Remember," Mr. Rissin continued, "I don't wish you good luck. Organization, knowledge, preparedness, proper technique, and accuracy are your tools for success. Any questions?" Keeran looked around the classroom. No hands were up. Everyone was ready and eager.

"All right then. Everyone to your lab station." Mr. Rissin waited until everyone settled in. "When the classroom lights flash you will have thirty minutes from that point to complete the qualitative analysis lab. All right, dig in everyone."

Immediately the lights flashed. First Keeran put her safety goggles on. Points could be deducted for not doing so. Then she began organizing her workspace: lab notes and note pad to the left, compound samples directly in front of her, and testing agents to the right. They were distilled water, anthocyanin, acetic acid, and iodine. She set up another test tube rack and filled it with eight, clean test tubes. She took one-third of the distilled water and poured it into a beaker. Keeran set up a stand with a ring clamp. She put a small screen on the ring clamp and the beaker on top of the screen. She placed a burner beneath it. Turning the gas on, she lit the burner with a striker. From experience Keeran knew hot water was sometimes needed for crucial tests towards the end of the qualitative analysis lab. Having hot water ready was a huge time saver.

Keeran began testing each compound with the most general test; the distilled water. Using a scoopula and a small scale, she carefully measured 5 grams of each sample putting them one by one in the clean test tubes. Using a pipette, she cautiously added the same amount of distilled water to each test tube. She put a stopper in every one and vigorously shook each test tube. After a moment, she determined that five of the compounds were soluble and three were insoluble. She arranged the soluble test tubes on the right of the test tube rack and the three insoluble ones on the left.

Scanning her lab notes, anthocyanin is best when testing soluble compounds. It is a flavinoid. Its pigments were water soluble. She took her pipette and carefully measured five milliliters and inserted that amount into each soluble compound. Keeran scanned the test tube rack to read the results. Test tube one was yellow-green, the second test tube was blue, and the third's color was violet. The fourth had no color change at all, and number five's color was grayish. Five test tubes out of four turned color; one did not. She decided to take a chance that two compounds must be in one test tube. She discarded the colorless test tube sample.

Checking her notes, she read that calcium carbonate turns yellow-green when introduced to anthocyanin, but that result was not conclusive. One additional test was needed to be sure. She opened the top drawer of her lab station and found an eye dropper. She filled it about half-full of acetic acid and introduced it to the yellow-green compound. Keeran held the test tube up to eye level and observed bubbles. All right, she thought, I have identified my first compound, calcium carbonate. She carefully wrote the compound name on her note pad.

Checking her lab notes, Keeran determined the blue test tube was sodium bicarbonate and the grayish compound was borax. No more testing required for those. Now she thought, let's see if I guessed correctly on there being two compounds in the violet test tube.

Keeran knew there were two compounds that turned violet when anthocyanin was introduced. They were sucrose and sodium chloride. However, sucrose was very soluble in hot water and sodium chloride was not. She put on heat-proof gloves and carefully poured 10 milliliters of the prepared hot water in the test tube. She stoppered the test tube and gave it several shakes. Most of the violet substance was in suspension while some had settled to the bottom of the test tube. Nice, she thought. She wrote down the results on her lab pad.

Three to go. Keeran reached for one of the test tubes designated insoluble. Pulling the test tube out of the stand she looked up to see the timer. Twenty minutes to go. Plenty of time, she thought. However, she temporarily lost her concentration and misjudged clearing the test tube out of the rack. The test tube bottom pulled on the outside of the hole and fell off of her fingers rolling around on the other side of the stand of hot, distilled water. Blocked by the stand, she could not reach the test tube in time. It fell on the classroom floor and broke in several pieces. There was an audible silence in the classroom. Then the students got back to work. Keeran's heart sunk. Mr.

Rissin will deduct points for broken lab equipment. She rushed to his desk to get a new test tube as he was writing down Keeran's infraction. She started the process all over again with this insoluble solution.

The anticipation and excitement of the lab had disappeared for Keeran. She would not win today and most likely fall out of first place. Then Keeran thought, don't let an unfortunate accident ruin the morning; there were two labs left after this one. With a new resolve she proceeded on. One of the insoluble compounds reacted to iodine with a deep blue color. The other two did not. She wrote down cornstarch on her lab pad. Rereading her lab notes, she tested the final insoluble substances with acetic acid. One compound created bubbles; calcium carbonate. The other did not; calcium sulfate. On a clean sheet of paper, she carefully wrote her findings when Trace stood up and briskly walked to Mr. Rissin's desk with his answers. He had finished first and would receive two extra points. He handed his answer sheet to Mr. Rissin. With shoulders slumped, Keeran let out a sigh.

When she had finally finished writing her answers, Keeran double checked them for accuracy and spelling. Satisfied, she walked up to Mr. Rissin's desk. He accepted Keeran's paper and quickly checked her answers for accuracy.

#1 Sodium Carbonate
Na2CO3
Washing soda

#8 Sodium Bicarbonate
NaHCO3
Baking soda

#3 Sodium Borate
Na2B4O7
Borax

#5 Sucrose*
C12H22O11
Sugar

#7 Sodium Chloride*
NaCl
Salt

#2 Amylose/Amylopectin
(C6H10O5)n
Cornstarch

#4 Calcium Carbonate
CaCO3
Limestone

#6 Calcium Sulfate
CaSO4
Gypsum

*Sucrose and sodium chloride were in the same test tube. Sucrose is more soluble than sodium chloride in hot water.

Time was up. All answer sheets were collected and quickly corrected by Mr. Rissin. "This was the highest collective score ever in a qualitative analysis lab," Mr. Rissin announced to the class. "That score is 97% accuracy." He congratulated everyone on a lab well done. Then came the results. The standings were projected on the wall behind Mr. Rissin's desk. Keeran scanned the names and scores; not much had changed. The ten chemistry students were within mere points of each other. And to her surprise, Keeran saw that she and Trace were still tied for first place. Trace had received two extra points for finishing first, but was deducted two points for an error in the chemical formula for sodium carbonate.

Keeran on the other hand, turned in a perfect answer sheet and earned two extra points. Unfortunately, her broken test tube resulted in a two point deduction. Well she thought, I'm still in an excellent position with two labs to go. Her spirits rose a touch.

After school she met with her friends for the walk home. Vyla looked at Keeran and said slyly, "You know Keeran, I think Trace likes you."

"What!? Why would you say that?" Keeran asked incredulously.

"Well, before the lab he came over to you to wish you good luck. During the lab I would occasionally look his way. I would find him watching what you were doing in the lab." Vyla continued, "And that mistake he made on the sodium carbonate formula wasn't like him. I think he may have done it on purpose to keep you close to him in lab points."

"That's ridiculous," Keeran said. "It sounds to me like you're the one who likes Trace." And Keeran thought, so Trace may like me. That was very interesting.

And so the conversation went with Keeran, Vyla, and Arris on the walk home.

I found myself sitting on iron-oxidized soil, Mars' soil. I sniffed the air; it seemed okay. I reached in the leather pouch for my clothes and began to get dressed; damn leather pouch. I stood up, dusted myself off, and began putting on my underwear. Pulling on my shorts, I suddenly felt dizzy. Struggling to get them up, I sat down to pull them on. With shorts secured, I labored to get socks and sneakers on my feet. I had fumbled tying the knot and making the bow on both shoes. I was short of breath and my heart began racing. I felt terrible. Geez, there's not enough oxygen in Mars' atmosphere to sustain me, I thought. I've got to get back to Phobos. If I had the strength maybe I could crawl and get inside the mist. I looked around the Martian land-scape. There was no mist.

With labored breathing, I lied on my back and realized that I'm probably going die on Mars. Suddenly I heard voices. I turned my head to hear which direction they were coming from. To my surprise, the voices were getting louder; a glimmer of hope. I could barely raise my arm, but began waving it. I tried to shout, but it came out as more of a groan. Then I saw feet and legs in front of me.

"Oh my god, what is it!?" Keeran shouted as she looked down at Mike.

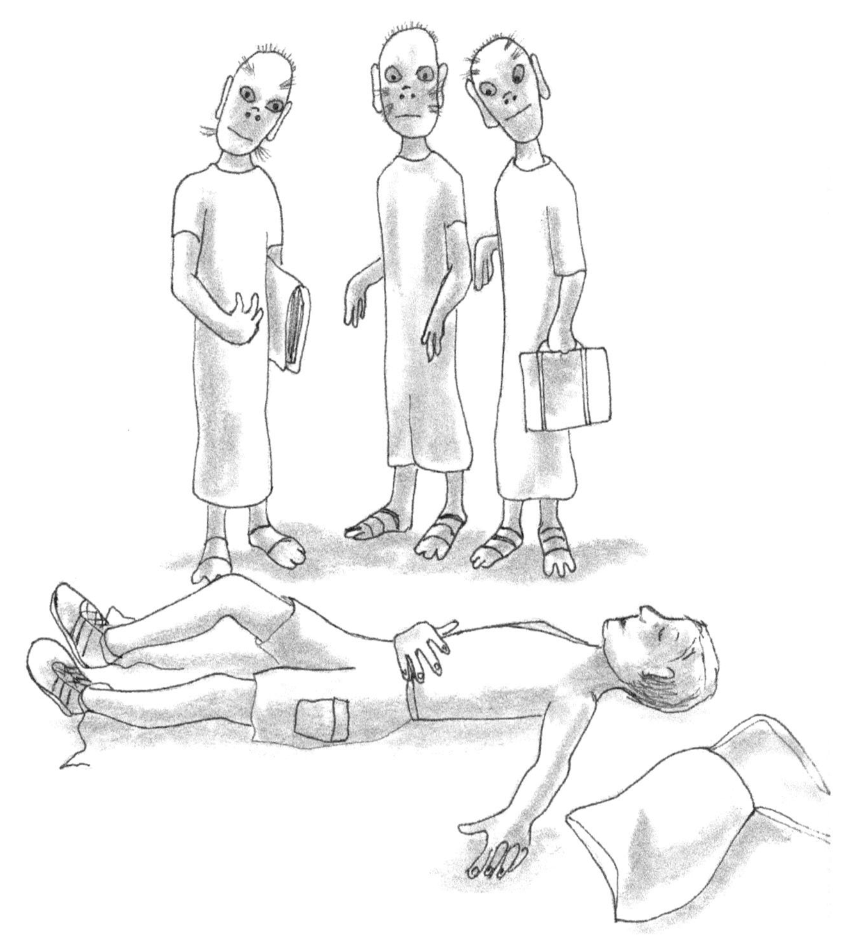

13

Commander Logan was escorted into the Oval Office and seated in a wooden chair with leather cushions in front of the president's desk. He was offered coffee, tea, and water. He declined all three thinking a double bourbon neat was more appropriate for this meeting. Logan had been in the Oval Office once before strictly as a military aide to his commanding officer. It never ceased to be a humbling experience being here, he thought.

Logan looked around the office. He knew John Adams was the first president to live in the White House as did every president since. The Oval Office was steeped in history as displayed by the many portraits of key figures throughout United States history. Thomas Jefferson, Benjamin Franklin, George Washington, Abraham Lincoln and more adorned the Oval Office walls. Along with the portraits the windows behind the president's desk were framed in gold curtains with the American and Presidential flags displayed on either side. The place reeked of power.

Startling Logan, the side door swung open as the president entered the Oval Office. Logan stood up, saluted and said, "Mr. President."

The president returned the salute and came right to the point as he sat at his desk. "Please sit Commander Logan. Your report on Michael McAlister." From the top drawer of the desk the president brought out a yellow legal pad and placed it in front of him. He took a pen from his suit coat pocket.

"Yes, sir," responded Commander Logan. "One of our objectives concerning McAlister has been met. We now know how he travels to the moon at extraordinary speeds. Somehow he has befriended extraterrestrials and they transport him to the moon in their spacecraft. Our other objective regarding time travel is still unknown. We do not know how he has the ability to travel back in time." Logan noticed that the president took notes the entire time that he spoke.

"Where is McAlister now?" the president asked. He had read Logan's preliminary report and knew exactly where McAlister was. Without accusing Logan of botching the mission, this request would serve the same purpose, the president thought.

"McAlister has returned to 1989 where he had built a log home in the early eighties," explained Logan. In other words, Logan thought, he escaped and I had failed the mission.

The president shifted a little in his chair and quietly said, "This is precisely why the Gruits was formed. You and your people work under the guise of the military, but operate independently and answer to no one but me since I do not have that luxury. So, where are we headed with this?"

A dressing down, thought Logan. "Sir, I firmly believe McAlister will return to me, I just don't know exactly when," Logan said.

"Why?" the president asked skeptically.

"You've heard of the Stockholm Syndrome. McAlister and I built a somewhat fragile rapport with each other until he escaped. We were on a first-name basis. The other reason I believe he will come back is he has no other place to go," Logan stated.

The president looked down at his yellow legal pad and wrote what Logan had said. The president thought, that makes perfect sense. Where else would or could he go?

"Please keep me informed immediately of any updates," the president commanded. They both stood, exchanged salutes and the president disappeared through the Oval Office side door. As the president left the Oval Office a presidential aide entered and ushered Logan out.

The three Martians stared down at me. "I don't know what it is, but it looks to be in distress, Keeran," Arris said anxiously.

"It keeps pointing to its mouth, then puts both hands on its chest," Vyla observed.

My sign language wasn't working, I thought. I need to change my strategy. With my right hand I mimed having a pen and in my left hand I was drawing on a paper pad.

Keeran said excitedly, "I think I've got it! It wants to write or draw something." She reached into her school supplies and produced a pen and paper notebook. She turned the pen on and handed both pen and notebook to me.

Taking them I drew eight small circles crowded together creating a nucleus. Then around the nucleus I drew two circles evenly spaced circumnavigating the nucleus. Lastly, I sketched six circles evenly spaced, but in a higher orbit above the nucleus. I handed the drawing back to the Martian.

Keeran looked at my drawing and shouted, "Oxygen! It needs oxygen for its respiratory system. I will be right back!" In Mars' reduced gravity, Keeran literally flew back to school.

The lab storeroom in the chemistry classroom was in the back. Keeran hurriedly entered and found a shelf that contained canisters of different gases. She grabbed one labeled oxygen, found some flexible tubing and ran back to her friends and the being.

My eyes were closed as I slowly lost my grasp on life. I couldn't remember where I was and didn't care, either. Then I felt something being inserted in my mouth accompanied by what felt like a fresh breeze going down my throat. I closed my lips around the tube and began breathing in slow, large breaths. I instantly began to feel better. I suddenly remembered where I was. Opening my eyes, I saw three beings looking down at me; Martians. One of them was kneeling by my left side. I held out my hand to it. I watched it look at the other two Martians and then back at me. It extended its hand into mine. I gave the Martian's hand a gentle squeeze and then let go. With a concerned look on its face, I saw it smile.

I was beginning to feel well enough to sit up. A struggle at first, I made it up into a sitting position. I looked at all three of my benefactor's faces. They were very similar; tall and slender with a somewhat elongated face, large brown-in-brown eyes, long narrow ears, and rather large nose nostrils. Their mouths were very wide with no lips. The Martian's heads had very short reddish hair and their skin was reddish-brown. It appeared they all wore the same clothing fabric, perhaps like a jute or hemp material.

The only differences between them was odd facial hair. The Martian on my right had two clumps of hair growing out of each side of its forehead. The one in the middle had two batches of hair growing on each cheek. The Martian on my left had four groups of hairs, one above each eye and one on each side of its lower cheeks; all about three inches long.

I noticed they were all communicating with each other, but it was extremely odd listening to their voices. I didn't hear any consonances, just vowels. Maybe they didn't have a tongue. The Martian kneeling next to me spoke and gestured with its hands and arms, opening them to the surrounding land. Its head slowly turned as it looked out at the vast distances. It pointed at me and repeated this gesture several times. Finally I thought, it must be asking me where I am from. I did the pen and paper meme again and it handed them to me. I drew the sun and all nine planets orbiting it. I pointed at the Martians and then pointed to the fourth planet. I motioned to myself and the third planet. Feeling strong enough I said, "I am an earthling."

The ETs stood in Mr. Wizard staring at the huge green crystal that Mike had entered. ~I am not experiencing Mike's presence,~ Rosie thought. ~He may have entered a hexagonal crystal plate to somewhere on Mars.~

~The hexagonal crystal plates have ceased to function since the cleansing event,~ thought Lumpy.

~It is possible to operate a plate transporting to a past time,~ thought James T. ~There have been two seismic events during Mike's duration in the green crystals. Perhaps there has been an unfortunate event.~

~This site is no longer sacred to us. We can enter these green crystals,~ thought Rosie.

Lumpy and Rosie descended from Mr. Wizard and carefully approached the green crystal that Mike had entered. Holding hands, they proceeded inside. Of the millions and millions of hexagonal crystal plates they saw only one was showing a scene of the Martian surface. Pointing at the plate, Rosie thought, ~Whether he chose to or not, Mike must have transported himself through this plate to the Martian surface.~

~With all the plates nonoperational but this one, Mike cannot return here,~ thought Lumpy.

~We must make all of the plates operational,~ Rosie thought. ~You, James T, Mr. Wizard, and I shall join together and maneuver time here in Phobos' crystals to return the plates to a functional status. Only then will Mike be able to come back here from Mars.~

The Martians and I walked along a dirt trail. Two of them said something and walked off together leaving me and my new friend by ourselves. I waved and said good bye. They stopped for a moment, looked at one another, then turned and kept on walking. The two of us continued along the dirt trail. I began seeing structures in the near distance. They were exactly what I had seen in the hexagonal plate in the crystals; reddish-brown circular buildings with dome-shaped roofs. I wondered what they were used for? Could these be their homes, I thought?

Just then my Martian friend backhanded my left arm and yelled, "What?!" We both stopped and looked at one another. "What did you say?!" the Martian asked excitedly.

It never occurred to me to use thoughts in trying to communicate with the Martians. ~I was wondering if these structures are your homes. Can you hear my thoughts with your mind?~ I asked. We continued walking on the dirt trail as we tried to communicate with one another.

Even though she kept talking in the strange language, its thoughts said, "Yes. I can hear your thoughts. How do you do that?"

~Oh, it's something I learned from friends of mine. So, what is your name?~

"I am Keeran. The rest of my family name is displayed on my face utilizing hair planted in different places, different styles, with different numbers of hairs. And do you have a name?" Keeran asked.

~You can call me Mike. It is very nice to meet you. I am so glad you know something about chemistry or I wouldn't be walking with you. Earth's atmosphere is about twenty percent oxygen,~ I explained.

~Chemistry is my favorite class at school,~Keeran said proudly.

~Thank god for me it is!~ I thought. ~ I'm curious Keeran, do you have different sexes, like male and female; men and women?~

"Yes, we do. I am a woman. Oh, here we are at my home," she said pointing at a reddish-brown silo-like structure. "And you were right. Almost all of these buildings are our homes. Please follow me to the plantation where my father is working. He will have a better idea about helping with your current situation here on Mars," she said.

Keeran led me around her home and to an entrance into the huge building I had seen through the hexagonal plate in Phobos' green crystal. With a wave of her hand, the glass door slid open allowing us to enter. It appeared we were walking into a type of holding room; very bare and about ten by twelve feet in size. As soon as I got inside, the door slid shut behind me. Another wave of Keeran's hand and I felt air of some sort rushing in. From a drawer that opened automatically from the adjacent wall, Keeran produced a small device that she inserted into her nostrils. The device barely covered her nose and the color was reddish-brown. You could hardly tell she was wearing it.

"I have flooded the airlock with the same atmosphere that is in the plantation building. I cannot breath it, hence this breathing device." She pointed at her nose. "However, you shouldn't need your oxygen canister now. This atmosphere mixture is what we use to grow our crops. It contains close to twenty percent oxygen, "Keeran explained.

I took the canister tube out of my mouth and began breathing normally. ~I think you're right Keeran. This air seems very acceptable to me, thank you,~ I thought. Along with my leather pouch, I put the canister on the floor next to the closest wall.

Keeran waived her hand again and the wall separating the air lock and the plantation became clear revealing different types of vegetation. My god! I thought. Look at all the plants, all the crops! I tried, but I couldn't even see to the other end of the building. It seemed to stretch on forever.

"Father," she called. "If you are close to the airlock, I have a situation you need to be aware of." Looking back at me Keeran said, "My father is the head horticulturalist of all these crops."

"All right Keeran," her father said. "I need to clean this area first and then I will see you at the air lock."

I asked Keeran, ~Are all of your crops grown indoors like this?~

"Yes. Everything we grow is indoors and is for our consumption or used in making our clothing." She looked down at her dress and held out a part of it showing me the fabric.

~Are all Martians vegetarians then?~ I asked.

"I don't understand your question," Keeran said with a skeptical look.

I tried to rephrase my question. ~Martians don't eat anything else but these crops?~ I pointed to inside of the plantation.

"What else would that be?" She motioned with both arms at the plantation. "This is what all Martians consume."

Just then, I saw her father come around the corner of some large bushes heading towards the airlock. He and Keeran's features were remarkably similar. Tall and slim with very little hair on his head, they both had the distinctive groups of hair on their faces; one above each eye and one on each lower side of their cheeks. Keeran's father had the same device covering his nose as Keeran. He entered the airlock, stopped abruptly, startled. He took a long look at me before addressing Keeran. "How did your lab go today?" he asked.

"It was one of my best. I scored a perfect twenty points and earned two extra points because of it. But, I dropped a test tube on the table and it rolled off, hit the floor and broke into several pieces. Because of that, I was deducted two points. I am still tied for first place with Trace though," she explained proudly.

"Congratulations Keeran," he said as he gave his daughter a hug. "Now," pointing in my direction, "please explain your involvement with the Offworlder." His expression and tone turned very grave.

Keeran thought, that was odd. I've never heard of that term Offworlder before. She proceeded to explain to her father about finding me along the trail coming home from school. She told about getting oxygen for me and saving my life. She decided that when I was able to walk, it was best to bring me here to the plantation and to her father.

"Keeran, you did the right thing," said her father.

"What will happen to Mike now?" she asked very concerned.

"Mike?! You know its name?" he asked, surprised.

"Yes. We have spoken several times with each other."

Keeran's father sighed. "Who else was with you today?"

"Arris and Vyla," she answered.

Her father took Keeran in his arms and gave her another hug. Then he gently put his hands on her shoulders looking into her eyes and said sadly, "You must now go in our home and do not return here today."

Keeran was confused and frightened. She had never seen her father act this way before. It was best to do as he said, she thought. She turned, looked at me one more time and left the air lock.

Keeran's father turned to me. "If you can understand me, I am truly sorry but there is nothing I can do for you."

Apprehensive and upset, I thought, ~What is going to happen

to me?~

"It will take place quickly. Please follow me outside," Keeran's father commanded.

He took his nose device off as we left the airlock. I gathered the leather pouch and oxygen canister. I wondered how much oxygen was left in it. Following Keeran's father outside, I saw several Martians heading in our direction. We stopped, evidently waiting for them to meet with us. They finally walked up to where we were standing. There were four of them. They looked to be two men and two women. Each had their own different groups of facial hair. They greeted Keeran's father and addressed him as Eath. Then they just turned and stared at me.

"Eath, please step aside," one of the men said. "As you are aware, helping an Offworlder carries a strict penalty. However, it has been decided to waive punishment of Keeran. We haven't had an Offworlder visit Mars in centuries. The old ways have not been taught, perhaps even forgotten by many of us. Our sons and daughters may not have learned about the past with Offworlders."

"Thank you prefect, said Eath bowing in the prefect's direction. "So that you are aware, the Offworlder can understand us by using his mind."

"Then we must not waste any more time," the prefect said hastily.

~Excuse me,~ I thought excitedly. ~I am here because of a mistake. I have been waiting for my transport to arrive so I may leave Mars. But it hasn't come yet. As soon as it does, I will leave Mars never to return.~

As if I had said nothing, the prefect continued in an authoritative voice, "As far back as Martian history remembers, Offworlders are associated with disease, pestilence, and plagues." As the prefect was going through his incantation, the other three Martians moved to form a circle around me. "The Offworlder must now be eradicated."

As I watched the Martians each one was in possession of reddish colored round objects in their hands, about the size of a golf ball. Except there appeared to be many small spikes protruding out of the them. Without warning the first ball hit me in the chest. I tried to pull it out, but I saw that each spike had a barbed hook on the end. I could not get it free. Then came the pain. Whatever it was, the spike deliv-

ered some kind of poisonous toxin that spread in my chest. The pain was excruciating. It felt as if my chest was on fire. I fell to my knees, moaning. Then another ball hit my back with the same result. The toxin extended throughout my entire back. I tried crawling away from the Martians and to Eath, but it was useless. Two more balls hit my legs. My muscles began to spasm. My entire body was shaking uncontrollably. I was in total agony.

The last ball thrown landed on my lower back. Having trouble breathing, I tried to crawl on my elbows to Eath. I felt myself losing consciousness. My last thought was to make a vague gesture to him. As I collapsed to the ground, I threw my right arm at his feet striking the Martian surface.

Eath returned home, sullen and distraught. Keeran was waiting for him at the sliding door. "Father, I have just researched the history of Offworlders. Why haven't you told me about this before? I don't think any of my friends know what this Offworlder legend is all about, either. Today I saved a living thing and now I assume that it is dead!"

The irony was not lost on Eath. He and his partner taught their daughter to respect all forms of life on Mars. Oh, if it could only be that simple, he thought. Eath looked down at his daughter and finally said, "Mike escaped."

"What!? How?" exclaimed Keeran excitedly. After her research she knew there was no escaping the poisonous red balls.

"After being hit by five red balls, Mike struggled to crawl over to my feet. He reached out his right arm to me as it struck the ground. Mike said to me, ~You have a beautiful daughter.~ And then, he just vanished."

Extremely relieved, Keeran asked, "Where do you think Mike went, father? Back to earth?"

"From wherever it came, I suppose. You now have an adventure no one else will ever experience; cherish it, Keeran." And for the third time that day Eath gave his daughter a hug.

14

Unconscious, I suddenly appeared at Rosie's and Lumpy's feet. Rosie looked at me and thought to Lumpy, ~Quickly, if we are to save him.~ 'Quickly' also applied to the ETs. Manipulating time required an extreme amount of energy. Because of this, all the ETs needed a period of inactivity to recharge. Carrying me, they exited the green crystal. As soon as we left, all of hexagonal plates went blank.

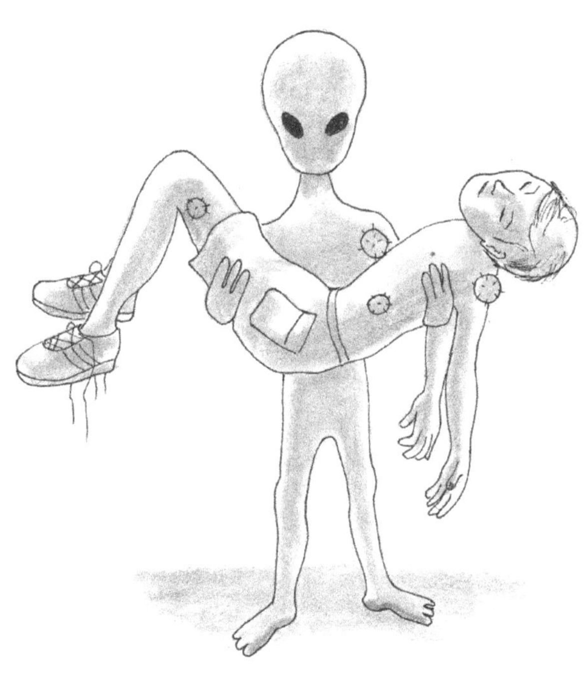

Below Mr. Wizard, Lumpy held me in its arms while Rosie operated with the dexterity of a brain surgeon. It removed the spiked red balls from my chest, back, and legs. Luckily, Lumpy didn't expend much energy holding me. Phobos' gravity turns 150 pounds into two ounces. They removed my clothes and all three of us returned to the inside of Mr. Wizard. After they gently laid me down on the deck, all of the ETs went into a time of inactivity. It was now up to Mr. Wizard to extract the poisonous toxin from my body and absorb it into its own. Being bio-engineered in a different dimension had its advantages or perhaps this time, disadvantages.

Several hours went by before my eye lids began to flutter. Disoriented and confused, I laid still for several minutes trying to gather myself. Finally with eyes wide open I moved my head back and forth looking at my surroundings. I was back inside Mr. Wizard, I thought. Thank god! I also saw James T, Lumpy, and Rosie. They were standing perfectly still. What's the deal with that, I thought? Then I remembered. They were probably in a sleep-mode while recharging.

My chest, back, and legs were extremely sore. I got up on my elbows. I felt faint, slightly dizzy, and thirsty. I struggled to get to my feet and walked unevenly to where my leather pouch was in the aft of Mr. Wizard. Realizing I couldn't drink water in the craft's medium I slung the leather pouch over my shoulder and packed it to the portal. I went down to Phobos' cavern floor. I took out one of the water bottles that young Mike had given me, opened it and began drinking. It was exactly what I needed to hydrate myself. Water never tasted so good.

When I returned to their craft, the ETs were active. Facing all of them I thought, ~I have no idea what you all did to get me off of Mars, back here in Mr. Wizard and recovering from the Martian's barbaric ritual, but thank you all so much!~

~We are relieved that you are well,~ thought Rosie.

~Before we move on I have a question. Why did all the hexagonal crystal plates in Phobos' green crystal stop at the same time? They were all blank.~

No response from the ETs. ~All right then, did all the Martians die at the same time?~ I asked. No response. From my association with the ETs, once again they were making this a learning experience for me.

~When you feel you are fully recovered there is one more mission required that you undertake. We believe you need to fully understand about the meaning of Phobos' crystals.~

~How much time has elapsed since we left the moon?~ I asked.

~Approximately eight hours,~ answered James T.

~Thank you,~ I thought, ~Rosie, first, where are we going? How rigorous is this experience and how long will it take? I've only got about two days before Kate and I need to meet with the librarian.~

~We will travel to the Martian surface. Walking is involved as well as observing. Time estimation is approximately two hours, ~ explained Rosie.

Let's see, I thought, two hours of walking and observing. How tough can that be? ~All right, if the excursion is completely necessary, I would like to go now. Time is very important.~

We immediately departed Phobos and headed down to Mars' surface. Once there we flew very low over the stark terrain. I began wondering what happened to all the buildings that I had witnessed in my brief visit to Mars' past. If all the hexagonal crystal plates stopped operating at the same time, did that mean there was a mass extinction of all the Martians? And how many years ago was that, I thought? Way more questions than answers at this point.

We slowed and came to rest on the Martian surface. The landscape was mostly flat consisting of reddish-brown sand. Rocks of various sizes were littered everywhere. Some of the ground resembled jagged, broken ceramic plates. There were two small mounds of sand and rock far off on either side of the craft.

Rosie thought, ~We have come to rest on an entrance to Mars' interior. It is similar to the moon's entrance, however this one is too small for our craft to negotiate. You will descend into Mars alone through this passage.~

Geez, this is not what I expected; I will be exploring Mars' interior by myself? I'm a touch claustrophobic and do not like enclosed spaces. ~Is there no other way?~ I asked apprehensively.

~Your discomfort will not last long once you arrive at the intended destination,~ Rosie thought.

Rosie was not making a very good case. ~How long will I be descending to wherever I'm going~? I asked nervously.

~Eight minutes. Perhaps close your eyes during the descent,~ Rosie thought.

~Thanks a lot,~ I thought sarcastically. ~Do I need clothes or is it the same medium that's in the moon and Phobos?~

~It is the same medium. You will not need clothes,~ was Rosie's answer.

~Okay, what do I do?~ I asked.

~Please stand in the middle of the portal on the Martian soil,~ Rosie instructed.

No sooner did I stand on Mars, I began descending into it. Alice in Wonderland, I thought? What awaits me down there? After a few moments of being very tense, I began to relax a touch. I couldn't see much; it was extremely dark. But my rate of descent was tolerable. I thought, what is it that's so important down there? Why were the ETs so insistent on me observing something in Mars' interior?

Soon I saw my surroundings becoming lighter. Then I looked down and found myself standing on a smooth surface bathed in green light. I was right in the middle of a dark circle that was about twenty feet in diameter. Glancing around it looked like the usual cavern of the moon and Phobos, but this one was so much larger than the moon's. I looked up and could not see any ceiling. Looking straight ahead, I couldn't see the other side of this cavern. It appeared to be miles and miles long. And the floor was perfectly flat. Then to my left I noticed what appeared to be structures of some sort. Were they what I'm supposed to be investigating?

I began walking in the structures' direction. I hadn't gone thirty feet when suddenly I was ankle-deep in water. What is with this, I thought? I backed out of the water and tried to make out the shoreline. It curved left to right towards the structures, but I'd have to walk around it for a ways. No wonder the floor appeared to be perfectly flat. It was one huge underground lake. I wondered, is this where all of Mars' surface water ended up?

Walking closer I saw that they weren't structures at all. They were stacks; stacks of cylindrical objects. As far as I could see in either direction, there were perhaps thousands of these stacks. It reminded me of the last scene in *Raiders of the Lost Ark* where there were thousands of wooden crates in a huge warehouse. I walked up to the first stack. The cylinders were more tube-shaped with rounded ends. Each tube was about eight feet long and two and a half feet wide. They were perfectly round from end to end. In each stack, the bottom row consisted of eight tubes lined up next to one another. The second row in the stack had eight tubes, but ran the opposite way. This pattern continued all the way to the top of each stack. Looking upwards, I counted twenty-five rows. There were two hundred tubes in each stack. And all stacks were about two feet apart from each other.

I walked around one of the stacks to see if there was anything unusual or different about any of the tubes. They all seemed exactly the same including being covered in dust. With my hand I wiped some dust off the top end of one of the tubes. I was astounded at what I saw. It looked like a window in the tube. Wiping it with my hand some more wasn't getting all the dust off. After three trips to the lake bringing back water in my cupped hands, I could see that it was indeed a window. It was about eighteen inches square.

Trying to see in the window by the dim green light was difficult. I kept staring at the window hoping my eyes would fully adjust to the pale light. Eventually I began to see the outline of an object. It was irregular in shape and contained many contours. I continued staring at the object. And then it struck me! The irregular object was the face and head of a Martian! It appeared to be perfectly preserved.

I fell back thinking, does every one of these tubes contain a Martian? And if so, what was the purpose in putting a Martian in thousands, if not millions of these tubes? To see if indeed there was a Martian in each tube I washed the dust off of two more tubes' windows and looked inside. Yes, it seemed they all contained Martian bodies. The last window I washed had a little better access to light. I looked closely. This Martian had a small chain round its neck with a medallion attached. The medallion had an insignia engraved on it. Seeing this I went back and checked the other two. They also had chains around their necks, but the insignia on their medallions were slightly different.

I walked back out to the lake and looked again at all the stacks of tubes, each one containing a Martian body. I don't get it, I thought. What was the purpose in doing this? Is this how Martians were buried? Perhaps. Different cultures on earth have different ways of attending to their dead. Is this what the ETs wanted me to see? It has to be. There was nothing else here in the cavern but water and tubes.

I made my way back to the dark circle and stood in the middle. I'm glad to be leaving. Geez, this place has given me the creeps! ~Rosie, I am ready to return!~ I thought. Instantly I began my ascent to Mr. Wizard.

Upon returning to the ETs ship, I sensed an odd excitement from them. ~Rosie, what was that down there? Was it a type of burial ground for Martians?~ I asked.

~What do you know so far concerning the earth's moon and Mars' moon Phobos?~ asked Rosie.

It sounded like Rosie wanted me to use a little deductive reasoning to come up with my own answers. ~Okay, the earth's moon is an observatory collecting data on every living thing on earth. This data is then stored in the large green Crystals inside the moon. The Crystals are managed by a being called the librarian.~ I stopped thinking for a moment, but no one interrupted me. So I kept on.

~Mars' moon Phobos functioned the same way as the earth's moon is now. The green crystals gathered and stored data concerning all living things on Mars. However, there are three differences: there is no librarian that I am aware of in Phobos, all of the hexagonal crystal plates appear to have ceased functioning at the same time, and there is no life on Mars anymore.~ I stopped; no reaction from the ETs.

~Continue,~ coaxed Rosie.

~Through a catastrophic event there was a mass extinction of all life on Mars. My assumption is that all Martians living at that time were put into those tubes. For what purpose, other than burial, I don't know.~

I looked at Rosie, Lumpy, and James T. If they knew the answer, no one was forthcoming. And then an idea hit me and I was suddenly very afraid and apprehensive. I got sick to my stomach and thought I might throw up. ~Is there going to be a mass extinction of all life on earth?~ I asked hesitantly.

~At a point in time, yes,~ informed Rosie.

I did not want to know the answer to my next question. ~When that happens will all humans end up in tubes, like in Mars?~

Rosie hesitated, but eventually thought, ~Yes. You see, Mike, the librarian and its race of beings are carnivores.~

15

David looked at his watch, 1:28 p.m. He typed 'McAlister' on his computer keyboard and the file came up on the screen. Just then Commander Logan walked into the Gruits' office at Joint Base Andrews. David and Rick, working at their computers stood at attention. "Back to work, please," Logan said calmly. He went to his desk, rolled out the leather chair, sat down and opened his computer. "David, status on McAlister," he directed.

David looked at his computer screen. "Current records indicate McAlister is still in the year 1989 at his log home in eastern Washington, sir," David informed the commander. David and Rick exchanged a quick glance at one another. They knew the meeting with the president had not gone well for Commander Logan. Ever since then, David thought, the commander's behavior was becoming increasingly compulsive concerning McAlister. This was the second day in a row when Commander Logan would arrive to this office at 8:30 a.m., 10:30 a.m. and 1:30 p.m. asking about McAlister's status. And it wasn't just checking and rechecking on McAlister. The commander's actions were becoming very predictable, almost obsessive.

Once he received the report on McAlister the commander would type something on his computer, print it out, stand at his desk and close his computer adjusting it to be precisely square with the desk top. The commander would then straighten his tie, pull his coat down, and slide the leather chair under the desk. After retrieving the printed paper the commander would say 'good work everyone' and leave. David looked at his watch again; precisely 1:35 p.m. Just like yesterday.

The blue dot became larger and larger. We were approaching earth. I was standing in the bow of Mr. Wizard staring forward. What am I going to do now, I thought? The librarian; it could be another century or two before we earthlings become canned sardines. Or it could be tomorrow. Seeing the librarian with Kate in a day and a half did not sound like a good idea. It might be in the mood for a snack. I can't go back to our home at Pine Creek considering other countries, foreign nationals, and terrorist organizations could be waiting for me. I could go to 1989, but that doesn't solve anything. I want our lives back the way they were three days ago, but I don't know what to do to accomplish that. Finally I thought, ~Well, what do you guys think?~

~We have heard your thoughts,~ Rosie revealed. ~We agree with all of your conclusions. But there is one option you still have available to you.~ Rosie quit thinking for a moment.

I looked at Rosie. ~What option might that be?~ I asked.

~Commander Logan,~ thought Rosie.

~Commander Logan?!~ I exploded. After what all of us had been through with him, especially losing Satchmo. I couldn't bear the thought. I waited a moment to calm down. ~Your reasoning?~

~He did keep you and Kate safe,~ Rosie thought. ~Even though Commander Logan has his own agenda we do not feel you have any other choice in this matter.~

I thought for a moment. I knew Rosie was right. I just didn't want to admit it. I really had no where else to go. ~Do you know where Commander Logan is?~ I asked.

The ETs put me down at Joint Base Andrews. No alarms sounded on the base as I descended through the portal. I reached in the leather pouch and pulled out my clothes. No sooner had I got dressed than a man in uniform asked me if I needed help. "Commander Logan, please," I requested.

"And who is asking for Commander Logan?"

"Michael McAlister," I said.

The uniformed man talked on his cell phone while two other armed officers surrounded me. After a brief phone conversation the uniformed man said to me, "This way, please."

The four of us walked at least ten minutes before we entered an ornately decorated office building built of brown stone with wood trim. The front desk directed us to the right hallway and up a flight of stairs. The next receptionist sent all of us to the left hallway towards the base runways. The last doorway was opened for me by the uniformed man as I entered with the armed officers on either side. The last secretary directed us through an inner office door to Logan's office. As I entered there was Logan standing just behind the door. He was alone.

I walked toward him as I said, "Commander Logan." He quickly turned and faced me as we shook hands.

"Michael McAlister." He looked at the two armed officers. "Gentlemen, please stand guard outside my office door." As they stepped outside, Logan closed the door after them. He directed me to a small leather couch as he pulled over his leather desk chair and sat opposite me. "What can I do for you today, Mike?" He had a some-what half smile on his face.

"For one, I am starving. The least you can do is treat me to a dinner out." I was not kidding. I couldn't remember the last time I had eaten.

"You dressed like that? What hamburger joint do you want me to take you to?" Logan asked sarcastically.

"After a shower you can loan me one of those gray suits, take me out to an expensive restaurant and then we will talk," I said insis-tently.

Logan reached in his coat pocket, turned his cell phone on and dialed a number. "Dinner for two, say," he looked at his watch, "9:00 p.m. this evening? Thank you."

With two Gruits in tow, we drove to Logan's home on Joint Base Andrews. A very modest two-story colonial design, the house was painted sky blue with dark blue shutters on all the windows. A large lawn led up to the home with five red brick steps leading to the front door. Once inside Logan led me to the main floor bathroom and I took a much needed and well-deserved long, hot shower. When I finished I pulled the shower curtain back to see a gray suit hanging on the hook inside the bathroom door.

After toweling off, I put the gray suit on. I couldn't remember the last time I had worn a suit. Could I still tie a tie? I put it around my neck and said the incantation; over, under, around, and through. Wow, it still worked. The tie was tied. I looked in the bathroom mirror at myself; not bad. I walked into the small living room as Logan deliv-ered an Old-fashioned for me. Speaking to Logan I exclaimed, "As Will Smith said, 'I make this look good.'"

Leaving Logan's home in a military car, I looked down the side-walk where it curved to the left into some shrubs and bushes. In the

dark shade I saw a few firefly's doing their best to find a mate. After a brief ride in Logan's government-issue car, we arrived at the restaurant precisely at 9:00 p.m. It was the Officer's Club.

Pomp and protocol were on full display as we were seated next to a white marble statue of an angel pouring water from a pitcher into a pool at her feet. Instantly a waiter came over to our table with menus. He took my cocktail order; Beefeater gin martini up with a twist. Logan ordered ice water. The two Gruits were standing a respectable distance from our table.

"Are they really necessary?" I asked.

"My compliments.....again. I have never had a hostage escape from me and the Gruits. Yes, they are necessary when concerning you," Logan explained. "By the way, we know that you have had the tracking device removed. How did you figure that out? And who is currently in 1989?"

"I would rather not answer either question, but if it interests you it hurt like hell having the tracking device removed," I said.

My martini arrived; cold, dry, and delicious. Looking at the restaurants' offerings, I was not interested in hors d'oeuvres or soups and salads. My eyes went straight to the main dishes. And one particular dish stood out to me. *Braised Short Rib: braised in red wine, house gnocchi, short rib reduction, tomato jam, foraged mushroom, heirloom carrot.* Gnocchi, reduction, jam, foraged, and heirloom; why add these words to describe foods that I and most people don't understand? Oh, well.

We ate our meal in relative quiet. The braised short rib was an excellent choice: meaty, flavorful, delicious. It took no time for me to devour my meal. As I finished eating it appeared to me that Logan was somewhat anxious. The plates were removed and Logan said, "I knew you would return, Mike."

"I guess in a way I did, too," I responded. "Where else was I going to go, Ryan?"

"So, what do you have for me?" asked Ryan.

"I've decided to show you what exists in the moon and what it represents." I already regretted saying that, but I needed a different view point in light of what I saw in Mars. I just didn't know how much information I was going to tell Ryan, yet.

"When are we going?" Ryan asked. He seemed a little apprehensive.

"How about when we return to your house tonight?"

16

We arrived back at Ryan's home after dinner. Followed by two Gruits, we got out of Ryan's car and walked up to his front porch. The evening was dark, chilly, and overcast. "Where will we meet your friends?" Ryan asked.

"Right here on your front lawn in about ten minutes. Is that satisfactory? I asked.

"Yes, sir," commented Ryan. "Is there anything I need to do to be ready?"

"Clothing is not optional, only organic material is allowed inside their ship," I explained.

Ryan stood there and stared at me. "You have done all your travels and heroics with the extraterrestrials completely naked?"

"That is pretty much true," I agreed.

"I have completely misjudged you," Ryan said apologetically, "I won't do it again."

The ETs and I discussed a few scenarios involving Commander Logan before they dropped me off at Joint Base Andrews. We all agreed that he be allowed to travel to and inside the moon. We're hoping to gain a new perspective of the current situation. Is there something he, the Gruits, and the military could do to put a stop to the librarian's end game? And would that assure the continued future of humanity?

I kept thinking about the ETs. It bothered me that they were getting involved in the human races' predicament. It appeared they worked for the librarian and its lofty experiment observing earth. It seemingly is their mission of being. And yet they showed me the eventual outcome for all Martians and more importantly, what is in store for human beings. Even so, I could feel there was something they were not telling me; it seemed there always was. In the future I was going to keep in mind what the ETs ulterior motive could possibly be, if there was one.

Looking at me Ryan asked, "Where are they?" I looked up at the pulsating pale green portal just a few feet above us. "You or me first?" I asked as Ryan looked overhead.

"I will follow you and the Gruits," Ryan said.

"Sorry, no Gruits. It's either you and me or it's a no-go," I informed him.

Ryan looked at me, then up at the portal, and finally he looked at the Gruits. "Please attend to our clothing and stand guard by the entrance to my home," he instructed as we shed our clothing. "We will return soon." Then looking at me, he said, " Mike, I will follow you into their ship."

I raised my arms and ascended into Mr. Wizard followed by Ryan. As soon as we were aboard, the ship immediately headed for the upper reaches of the atmosphere and the moon. I introduced the ETs to Ryan. "Ryan, I would like you to meet my friends. Here is Rosie, this is Lumpy, and over there piloting the ship is James T." Silence. I was surprised that there was not an initial response between them. Finally, Ryan spoke, "Thank you for including me in your spacecraft for the brief flight to the moon." Several seconds went by before Rosie thought, ~Your attendance is welcome.~

Ryan was silent staring ahead at the growing moon. I thought he would have several questions concerning Mr. Wizard: what is this medium inside the ship? How do I breathe in this? Where are the ship's controls? Why aren't we subjected to the Laws of Motion and Gravity inside their spacecraft? What is the ship's propulsion? No, he continued in silence.

As we raced towards the crater entrance, I watched Ryan for his reaction. Is he thinking, are we going to stop or are we going to crash inside this crater? He had no reaction, not even a blink as we flew through the hologram of the crater's floor. Geez, he must have ice water for blood, I thought. His commitment is total on this mission and at all times, it seemed.

As Mr. Wizard entered the huge cavern it began to slow down as we approached the towering green Crystals. James T brought us to a stop and we all disembarked their ship. As a group we walked to the stone wall surrounding the Crystals. Stopping, everyone looked up at them. After a few moments, Ryan turned to me and asked, "Have you been inside?

"Yes," I responded.

"Please describe it to me," Ryan requested. His voice was very business-like.

"First, I believe that I enter the Crystals on a molecular level. Inside are diamond-shaped corridors that extend farther than the eye can see. On the corridor walls are small hexagonal-shaped crystal plates, about the size of a credit card. The plates' arrangement reminds me of a bee hive's honeycomb. There must be trillions and trillions of them throughout the Crystals ," I explained.

"How do you accomplish time travel?"

"It's more of picking a place that you want to visit in the past. Remember, everything and everyone has a crystal plate."

"Please, how do go back in time?" Ryan kept insisting.

"Okay, there are two ways. The first one is just touching a crystal plate. As soon as you do, you are immediately transferred to that place and time. The other way I discovered by accident. My first time in the Crystals I was trying to find Stonehenge. But in all of the trillions of crystal plates, where am I going to find Stonehenge's individual one? I just kept looking at one plate thinking of Stonehenge when the stone age structure appeared in the plate. Touch along the left side of the plate and things go back in time. Touch the right side and the plate advances eventually to its rightful time; pretty simple."

"And there's one more thing you should know, Ryan. The Crystals are operated or managed by a being from hell. It calls itself a librarian. It is vile, reprehensible, and evil. If you are not quick enough in your travels back in time, it will toss you in a black void; no way out and no determining when you will get out, if ever."

Nodding his head Ryan said, "All right. Thank you. I'd like to go back to earth now."

The trip back to earth was traveled in silence. As we hovered over Ryan's lawn, he and I descended from Mr. Wizard. The Gruits ran over with our clothing. Once dressed, I was ushered into Ryan's home. Evidently I was still under house arrest, I thought. In the stark living room Ryan invited me to have a seat on the brown leather couch. "I'll be right back," he said. On his return he brought two Old-fashioneds for us, handing one to me. As I took a sip he sat in the leather chair facing me. "I've been there before," he said matter-of-factly.

"What?! Where?!" I gasped.

"Inside the moon." Ryan had this far-away look in his eyes.

"What are you talking about? When was this?" I couldn't believe what I was hearing.

He looked at me and took a sip of his Old-fashioned. "I was twelve when the EBEs came to my bedroom offering me the universe if I would just go with them. Mike, I wanted to go, and I did."

"I can't believe you went with them?!" I said incredulously. "When I was nine-years-old they came to the bedroom where I was staying and scared the hell out of me. I went running and screaming into my aunt's living room twice that night!"

"Mike, let me explain. I took a sociology class in college. One of the things we studied was at-risk families. I suddenly realized then that my younger brother and I had grown up in an at-risk family. My father was pursuing a military career which meant we moved many times and attended many schools growing up. His commitment to the military, particularly the Navy, was paramount. He rarely had time to be a father.

My mother was left trying to raise two rambunctious boys. She smoked too many cigarettes and it seemed there was never enough money in our home. There was no physical abuse, but plenty of verbal abuse. It appeared that my parents always argued and fought about money, or lack there of. Then mom died in her early forties leaving my brother and I to take care of ourselves." Ryan stopped talking for a moment, perhaps lost in memories. But then he continued.

"The children of at-risk families have labels. Mine was the scapegoat, or black sheep. It seemed no matter what I did, our family's problems were my fault. I tried to be as honest as I could with my parents, you know, trying to impress them by telling the truth. That just seemed to make matters worse. Even my younger brother stayed away from me. He feared my parents might think he was associated with me."

"My little brother Karl's label was the lost child. He purposely stayed in the shadows trying not to be seen. And pretty much he succeeded, then and now. I haven't heard from nor seen him in years. I have no idea where he is or what he's done with his life."

Silence. After a couple sips of his drink, Ryan continued, "Anyway, I wanted out of our family and the EBEs offered me a way." Ryan was speaking softly, sullenly, but with conviction. I'd never heard him sound so vulnerable.

"What happened? Did you stick with the ETs or what did you do?" I asked. This whole conversation about our individual experiences with the ETs many years ago was very interesting, but also odd at the same time.

Ryan continued in a soft tone. "They asked me what I wanted to do first. I said, 'Take me to the moon.' And they did, perhaps trying to impress me. We went inside the moon to witness the green Crystals. But instead of experiencing and enjoying all the things that they had promised, I woke up the next morning in my bed and never saw them again. I was back to being the scapegoat of the family."

Ryan stared into his drink and was silent. After a couple of minutes I said, "Ryan, I didn't just come back for you to protect Kate and me from all the bad people in the world. There's way more that you need to hear. I am here to enlist you in helping save humanity."

Ryan looked up from his drink and asked, "What are you talking about? How on earth can I help save humanity? What haven't you told me?"

After a swallow of my Old-fashioned, I began describing the librarian, its seemingly supernatural powers, the black void where it resides, and the supposedly benign experiment of observing and recording a sentient race of beings.

And then I told him of my experience in Mars' moon, Phobos, and what's buried under the Martian surface. And that the same fate awaits all earthlings.

17

I was awakened at 5:00 a.m. Two different Gruits were standing guard at my bedroom door. Fresh clothes were delivered: a short-sleeve light sweatshirt, light brown cargo pants, white sweat socks, and white sneakers. My Gruit suit had been taken away. Once dressed I was escorted downstairs to the kitchen. Like the rest of the house the kitchen was stark. The walls were white as were the cabinets. The Formica counter tops were white as was the porcelain sink. In the small kitchen nook off to the right side, I sat at a small white table with three white chairs. Scanning the walls, there were no pictures, paintings or the usual ceramic trappings. I felt like I was back in the interrogation room; not a very good memory.

A light breakfast was served: fruit, granola with milk, toast, jam, and coffee. Once the breakfast dishes were cleared away, I walked over to the counter where the coffee pot was. As I refilled my cup Ryan entered the kitchen. He had his gray suit on, clean shaven with his hair impeccably combed. "Good morning, Mike. I hope your breakfast was acceptable. I want to apologize for my conversation last night. It was not my intent to discuss family matters."

"No need. I do understand," I said.

Ryan poured himself a cup of coffee as he said, "Thank you. I have called a general meeting of the Gruits this morning. We are going to discuss the situation in the moon that you described to me last night. I want to come up with a solid and viable plan to combat this librarian. Once we do, I will meet with the president for hopefully, final approval."

I thought to myself, doesn't something of this magnitude go before the Joint Chiefs of Staff, or some bipartisan congressional committee? And what are the Gruits anyway, some independent arm of the presidency? If so, they appeared not to have any checks and balances on decisions and actual procedures. How dangerous was that?

"Mike, you may be called upon to speak as the expert witness in this matter of national security, since you are the one with first-hand knowledge."

"If you think I can contribute positively to the decision-making process, I am fine speaking in front of the Gruits organization. Or I can wait somewhere while you and your colleagues determine a course of action," I explained.

"I'm sorry, Mike, but you are not leaving my sight," Ryan said firmly.

We drove to Ryan's office. After descending ten floors in the elevator, I was escorted by two Gruits to a small auditorium. It was completely white inside. I saw that it comfortably contained at least fifty chairs. They were lined up in perfect rows with a podium facing the chairs. In the back of the auditorium was a small white table and chair. There was only one way to the seats and that was through the door to the right side of the auditorium. As I entered through the door there was a grocery-like scanner on the left side. On the other side stood a tall white stand with a brown leather-bound small book entitled *The Mandate* laying on top. When we cleared the doorway I was escorted to the small table in the back and instructed to sit down. The guards stood back and on either side of me.

And then, like a procession with purpose Gruits began lining up to proceed through the doorway and to a chair. The men and women were mostly young, fit, and had the intent look of commitment on their faces. A few were older with wise expressions of experience and knowledge. Entering through the doorway, they placed their left palm on the scanner. After hearing the scanner's approval beep they would then place their right hand on *The Mandate* book. With eyes closed each Gruit would bow their heads for several seconds before moving to find a seat. It appeared like a cult ritual to me. Once all the Gruits were seated the lights lowered giving the effect of the Gruits being an entity of one. Lastly, Ryan entered the room. He stood by the side of the podium. More of a command than a statement, Ryan said, "Doctor, if you will, please."

A Gruit from the back row walked over to me with a small black bag. "Please put your forearms on the table. I am going to administer a small dose of a sedative in your arm. You will be asleep for the duration of Commander Logan's speech." Speech, I thought?

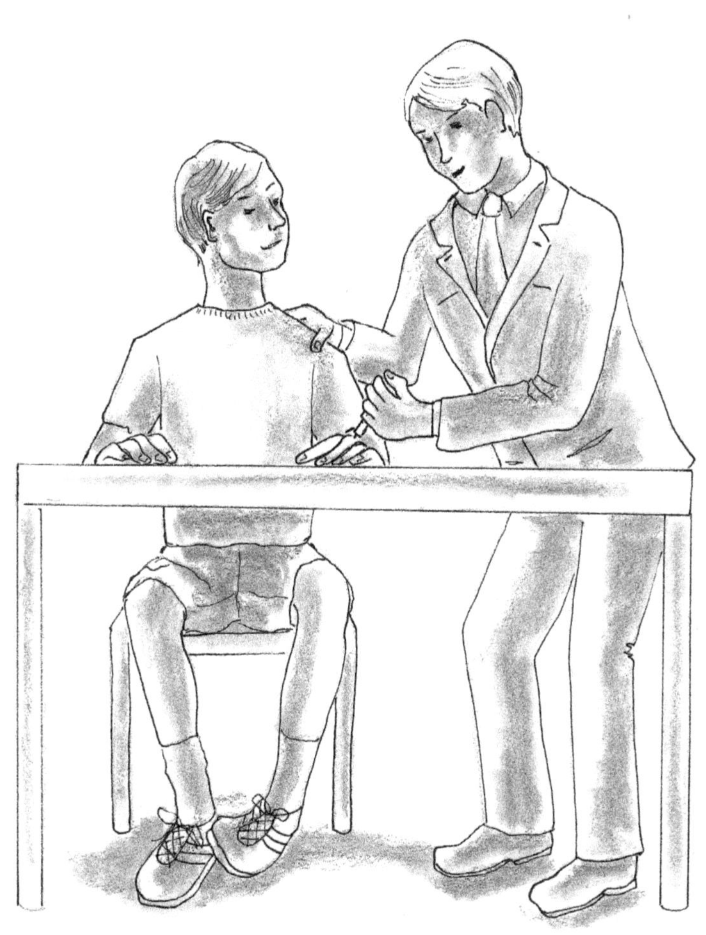

Wasn't there going to be a discussion about the moon and how to handle the librarian? What happened to me participating in the decision-making process?

I put my forearms on the table as the doctor instructed. He placed his small black bag beside my right arm. He opened it, reached in and pulled out a cell phone. He set it on the table inside my right arm. On the cell phone was a small piece of masking tape with the letters 'RECORDING' written on it. It was out of sight of my guards. Next, the doctor produced a syringe in his right hand, a ball of cotton and an alcohol swab in his left. After rubbing the inside of my right forearm with the alcohol swab, he placed the cotton ball by some veins and inserted the needle into the cotton. Pressing the syringe plunger, all of the sedative went into the cotton, none in my arm. He put the cotton ball and syringe back in his bag and gave my shoulder a small squeeze with his left hand. The doctor gently pushed my head on top of my forearms, closed his black bag and went back to his chair.

What is going on, I thought?! I didn't know what was happening, but decided to play along with whatever the doctor was up to. I pretended to be unconscious.

When the doctor sat down, he gave a short wave to Commander Logan. Commander Logan then stepped in back of the podium. He examined the room as if looking into every Gruits' eyes. His hands slowly rose and held each side of the podium. He had no notes or script. "My fellow Gruits," he began, "We are gathered here to celebrate a truly momentous occasion in the history of our organization's existence. Through calculated risk, precision planning, perseverance, hard work, and a wee bit o' Irish luck, I am informing you that we are on the threshold of completing our organization's Mandate." He paused allowing that statement to be fully absorbed by every Gruit.

Logan continued, "First, the wee bit o' Irish luck." My god, I thought, he sounded almost giddish. Where was that morose mood from last night and this morning talking about his childhood and growing up in an at-risk family?

"On Whidbey Island in Washington state, a local law enforcement officer's forensics established Michael McAlister's fingerprints on the local Lutheran church door knob and light switches. A concerned church neighbor investigated and took a somewhat blurry photo showing the backside of McAlister entering an extraterrestrial biological entities spacecraft," Logan explained. Then he pointed to a Gruit in the front row. "Bill, here, first made contact with McAlister a few weeks later and planted a tracking device into McAlister's shoulder. From monitoring the tracking device, we learned that McAlister and his EBE friends traveled to the moon. He did this feat in just three minutes. And not only to the moon, but inside the moon. From there, he traveled back in time to 1989 for approximately twelve minutes. That was when we decided McAlister could be a potential threat to the security of the United States."

"A few days ago, five Gruits and myself drove to McAlister's home to apprehend him. He did not come willingly. Unfortunately, Steve took the brunt of McAlister's fury and we eventually had to taser him. That afternoon we also apprehended his wife."

"Since our initial meeting with McAlister at his residence he was very uncooperative. We decided to take a calculated risk. You are all aware of the Stockholm Syndrome. It is a theory that tries to explain why hostages sometimes develop a psychological bond with their captors. So, we staged three attacks on us and McAlister. We blamed each attack on hostile entities interested in capturing McAlister with his newly acquired talents. Those entities were foreign governments, foreign nationals, and terrorist organizations. Of course none of that was true. But eventually McAlister began to believe that part of our mission concerning he and his wife was keeping them safe. McAlister and I soon began a first-name based relationship."

"However, we had our setbacks," Logan told his audience, "and had to persevere for a few days. Somehow McAlister figured out that there was a tracking device planted in his shoulder. With the help of his EBEs and two of their spacecrafts, McAlister and his wife were able to escape. They traveled to the moon and went back in time to 1989. But he was faced with a dilemma. Staying in 1989 did not solve anything for he and his wife in the long-term. He certainly couldn't return to his home in Washington state for fear of being captured by hostile forces. McAlister realized he had only one place to go and that was to return to us for protection. I am assuming his wife is still in 1989 with the tracking device."

"Last night was the coup de grace and our breakthrough. McAlister and I began sharing an experience we each had with the EBEs in our youth. I quickly turned the conversation into my horrible years growing up in an at-risk family. You all know my family. Nothing could be further from the truth. But McAlister took the bait and has agreed to help us. He just doesn't know he is assisting us to realize our Mandate. Yes, Gruits members, by hard work we were finally able to win over our very worthy adversary."

"Fellow Gruits, here are our findings. The moon is a huge data collecting device. Somewhere inside the moon are over fifty six-sided green crystals the size of Chicago skyscrapers. Enclosed in each are trillions upon trillions of hexagon crystal plates no bigger than a playing card. Every living thing is recorded in these plates. Each one of us has their own plate recording our daily history. McAlister can access these plates and travel back in time. He has agreed to train a squadron of Gruits to enter the Crystals to access the past."

"Meanwhile, a select committee of Gruits has investigated event time streams throughout our history. The committee has identified several key moments in those streams. If subtle changes are made to those moments, they would change certain aspects of United States history and American society."

"Imagine if you will an America where homelessness, poverty, and wealth do not exist, but prosperity for all. An America where there are no state boundaries, only geographical regions. Political parties are nonexistent. There are no elections; only citizen committees governing each region. Becoming a committee member would be by lottery participation."

Commander Logan's voice was reaching a crescendo in volume and strength. He became animated with his hands and arms. "Think of a society with no rules, no laws, no courts, and no lawyers. We no longer would be protecting the environment, the environment would be protecting us! And how would this be achievable and sustainable? The foundation to this new America would be life-long education!"

"Yes, fellow Gruits, we are going to realize our Mandate soon; the complete dismantling of our current American society and rebuilding it one section at a time until all of our goals for the new American society have been met. Only then can we truly move forward to finish our Mandate. With America as our shining example we can then change and manage the entire world!"

"And by making subtle adjustments to these historical time streams, no one will be the wiser. Change will take place without anyone knowing. It will all just happen." Logan paused for a moment letting the implications become apparent to the Gruits. In a crescendo, Commander Logan concluded, "I salute you, Gruits, for your patience and resolve. The day is finally here and it is ours!"

With his speech ended, Commander Logan saluted his fellow Gruits as the lights in the room brightened. The Gruits stood up as one and shouted loudly in unison, "Yes, sir!" They then marched out of the room. The doctor came over to me, opened his black bag and removed a syringe and vial. He filled the syringe with a clear liquid. Rubbing my right arm with an alcohol swab, he pretended to inject my arm as before. He picked up the cell phone and dropped it into his bag. "Lay still for a couple of minutes and then come to," he said in a whisper. "You should act groggy for awhile." He turned and disappeared into the Gruits crowd.

I sat there stunned beyond belief. My god! All the attacks were staged, I thought!? I rubbed my forehead. It was still sore from the first alleged attack. No foreign governments, no foreign nationals, and no terrorists groups were after Kate and me. And even though the whole time I was in captivity, I felt I was resolved and resilient concerning Logan. I trusted him, but fell for his charade.

As I thought back it all started with Logan's voice. It was strong, authoritative, calm, and reassuring. I first heard it when I was tasered. Logan instructed a doctor to knock me out. I heard it again during the first attack when Logan calmly instructed the counter-attack against the fake enemy. And then with each interrogation, Logan's voice became almost mesmerizing. Yes, he was right. I eventually swallowed both the bait and the hook.

And what about the librarian; the vile, contemptible being that could initiate a whole-scale extinction of all human life on earth at any time? That was the only reason I divulged all the information about the Crystals and time travel to Logan, to get Logan's and the Gruits' expertise in neutralizing or eliminating the threat from the librarian.

I sat at the table feeling extremely foolish. How stupid could I have been? Life-long education, Logan said. It will be more like life-long indoctrination. The Gruits were no more than a sad, misguided cult with Logan as its supreme, misplaced leader.

Slowly lifting my head I began looking around the empty auditorium. All the Gruits were gone including Logan, the doctor and my guards. What is this all about, I wondered? Logan said he was going to keep me in his sights at all times. Then the auditorium's door opened and two military men entered and walked over to me. Their uniforms suggested they were Marines: white peaked cap, midnight blue coat with red trim, standing collar, and a white web belt. The pants were royal blue with vertical red strips, and black socks and shoes.

"Please stand up Mr. McAlister," one of them ordered. I did as I was told. With white-gloved hands, one Marine handcuffed me and put the keys in his left coat pocket. The other Marine shackled my ankles.

18

I hobbled into the White House's Oval Office with the two Marine guards on either side. The presidential aide instructed us to please have a seat on the couch that was facing the president's desk. Once seated I couldn't help but look around at all the portraits of past presidents and other American historical figures. Paintings of battle scenes and events depicting American history were displayed in the back and to the right of the presidential desk. The desk itself looked to made of a deep, dark mahogany wood. On the left side of the desk was the American flag and the Presidential flag standing on the right side. The desk and flags were framed in by the gold curtains around the windows in back. Even the Marines joined me in scrutinizing the surroundings and trappings of American wisdom and strength inside the Oval Office. Even though the Oval Office was showing its age; plaster walls and ceiling with hairline cracks here and there while the wainscoting had wear marks where all the doors were located, it was all decorated to exemplify presidential power.

The Constitution provides the president with the authority to manage the many facets of American government. From faithfully executing laws passed by Congress, managing the executive branch, acting as Commander in Chief to Congressional veto powers and having sole responsibility of the Nuclear Authority are just a few of the president's responsibilities. But presidents can also wield tremendous powers that are implied. For example, using the 'bully pulpit' or conducting 'fireside chats' can be utilized to persuade public opinion in their favor. The Fourth Estate, the American media, can be used as a powerful tool to articulate the presidents' domestic and foreign agendas.

Whether trying to crack the whip without making a sound or having the appearance of grace, charm, and elegance cloaking iron and steel, the president's success will ultimately be decided on political leadership, managing legal boundaries, and gaining and maintaining the public trust.

One of the Marines adjusted his position on the couch reminding me of my current situation. Why am I here of all places, I thought? As if reading my mind the door next to the presidential desk opened as the President of the United States entered the Oval Office. Dressed in a dark blue suit with a white shirt and red tie, the president cut a formidable figure standing at six feet, three inches tall. It was well known that he exercised regularly. At fifty-eight years of age his rugged good looks were accented by a full head of hair with wisps of gray.

Both Marines stood, came to attention and saluted their commander-in-chief. The president smartly returned the salute and said, "Thank you gentlemen for bringing Mr. McAlister to me. Please wait out in the hall. This won't take long." The president also possessed 'the voice'. The Marines looked at one another, but quickly turned and exited the Oval Office.

The president pulled the chair out from under his desk and sat down. He opened the top drawer and produced a yellow legal pad and pen and set them on the desk top in front of him. He looked up and stared at me for a long time. I returned the stare. Finally he said, "Mr. McAlister, we finally meet. I can't say that it is a happy occasion. I believe you have been more trouble than you are worth. Time will tell. I am a patient man." He paused and wrote something on his legal pad. Then he continued.

"Dr. Fleming has given me his report."

"Don't you mean your mole?" I interrupted.

He stopped talking, lowered his eye brows and cocked his head a touch while looking at me. "Very good. When did you figure that out?" he asked.

"I had some time to think on the way over from Joint Base Andrews," I answered.

"Without some checks and balances, you can't be too careful with a military organization that is only responsible to the president. For your information, Commander Logan and the Gruits have been taken into custody for conspiring to commit treason against the United States of America and you are an accomplice to this heinous act."

"I willfully helped the doctor record Commander Logan's address to the Gruits. How am I an accomplice?" I demanded.

"Guilt by association," the president said calmly.

Just then an officious looking woman came through the side door by his desk. "Sorry to interrupt, sir, but the phone call you have been expecting is on Line 2."

The president looked up at the woman, "Thank you." To his left, he pushed the button on his phone and said, "This is President Logan."

Oh, my god! It finally hit me! I knew the president's name, but it took hearing it to make all the dots connect. I've watched President Logan's career for some time: military man, congressman, senator, and finally his run for the White House. And, of course, he has two sons. Thanks to the good doctor and me, he just arrested his own son, Ryan, for treason! Did he feel any remorse or sadness in doing so? What a world politicians must live in?!

The president finished his conversation and hung up the phone. Deep in my thoughts about the president and his family, I didn't see the Marines return, now standing on either side of me. President Logan picked up the yellow legal pad and pen and placed them back in the desk's top drawer. He stood up and said to me, "I don't know what I am going to do with you, yet; you and your acquired special abilities. In the meantime, guards, please escort Mr. McAlister to the military prison that was discussed about earlier."

Once again President Logan saluted the Marines as they returned the salute. Grabbing me under my arms they lifted me off of the couch and on to my shackled ankles and feet. As the president walked to the side door by his desk, he turned to me and said, "Have a nice time in military prison," and then continued walking towards the door.

With a loud voice I responded, "Mr. President, do you know where your son, Karl, is?"

As his face visibly reddened, the president turned towards us and shouted at the Marines, "Get him out of here!"

As we made our way through the White House, I was something of a spectacle in handcuffs and shackles escorted by the two Marines. Hushed tones greeted me in hallways and side doors until we finally made it outside. The three of us climbed into a black Suburban, one Marine driving and the other Marine in the back seat with me. I was seated on the left side and thought I heard the Marine say, "Cinch up your seatbelt tightly."

I turned to him and asked, "What did you say?"

He looked back at me and replied, "I didn't say anything."

Mmmm. I tightened my seatbelt until it almost hurt.

We drove out of Washington, D.C. on 410 heading southwest. Off of 410 we took the Arlington exit onto 82. There must be a Marine correction facility located somewhere in Arlington, I thought. Soon we left 82 and drove into a rural area. After another ten minutes driving on county roads we pulled up to a guard post. Perhaps the entrance to the correction facility, I thought. A young woman in her Marine uniform stepped out of the booth and with a big grin and bigger salute, watched as the Suburban went through the gate. As we passed her, I couldn't help myself. With cuffs on my wrists, I raised my arms and saluted back. She didn't flinch one bit and finally ended her salute as we were well passed her and the entrance gate.

We continued on a paved road through a wooded area. I was

looking out the passenger window to my left as we drove by a small ravine. The thought, ~Brace yourself~, entered my mind. I quickly lowered my head and put my hands and arms on the back of the driver's seat in front of me. The impact on the right side of the Suburban was sudden, loud, and swift. A large military truck struck the right side of the Suburban. The force of the collision sent the SUV crashing through the guard rail on the left side of the road. It began tumbling over and over until it reached the bottom of a large ravine. Having braced myself and closed my eyes, I could feel and hear debris flying around in the Suburban. It finally came to a stop resting on its right side.

In a daze, I looked around in the cab and at my fellow passengers. The driver was slumped to his right and not moving. The Marine next to me seemed to be knocked out with blood oozing out from a cut on his forehead. I could smell gasoline. I searched his left coat pocket and found the handcuff keys. With some doing I unlocked the handcuffs.

~Open the door window and climb out of the vehicle.~

I fumbled at the window button. To my surprise, it was still operating. I opened the window all the way down. I released the buckle on my seat belt. Holding on to the driver's seat headrest with both hands, I used the Marine in the back seat as a stepping stool. I crawled up through the left door window exposing my head, shoulders, and arms to the outside. Next, I positioned my hands on the passenger door and lifted my hips, legs, and feet completely outside the Suburban. I slid down the door some and then jumped into the brush below. The shackles made keeping my balance almost impossible as I did a forward shoulder roll into the brush when I hit the ground.

There was dust still settling from the collision after the SUV had rolled down the sidehill. I looked around in the ravine. It was covered with small brush and grass; some alive and some dead. On my hands and knees I began crawling up one of the ravine's steep sides. As I advanced my way upward I heard some popping and snapping noises from the dead brush underneath me. Suddenly, it felt like one of the branches had penetrated the inside of my left thigh. There was a pinching sensation. I looked down at my leg. I didn't see anything at first. Then blood from my inner thigh quickly began staining my pant leg. I could see a small hole in the fabric. A searing heat started to spread from that hole throughout my entire left leg. Soon all of my pant leg was drenched in blood. Whatever penetrated my leg must have hit a main artery or vein, I thought.

What sounded like someone snapping one of the dead branches, a bullet narrowly missed my chest and slammed into the hillside by my head. Dirt and debris flew into my face and eyes making me temporarily blind and vulnerable to more gunshots. I tried to move so I wasn't a stationary target, but my left leg would not cooperate. The loss of blood was causing me to become dizzy and light-headed. The pain in my leg became too much to bare. As I felt myself losing consciousness, a familiar voice thought, ~All right Mike, here we go,~ as I was lifted into its arms. I turned my head to see who it was. Through scratchy, blurry eyes I thought I saw a familiar face. The last thing I remembered before passing out was saying, "Satchmo?! Satchmo? Satchmo!"

19

Eyes opened, I found myself lying on my back, a familiar position lately. I stared at the ceiling for awhile trying to get my bearings. Eventually I turned my head to each side. I was lying on a bed in the middle of a small room. The ceiling, walls and arched doorway were a light cream color. They appeared to be made of concrete. The room was open to a hallway. There was no door. The ceiling was very low as was the top of the arched doorway. I touched the bed I was lying on. It was rock-hard, but somehow felt extremely comfortable. Everywhere there was a pale green light, but I couldn't see its source. The light just seemed to illuminate from the room's surroundings.

I sat up on my elbows and tried to think of how I got here. I remembered being transported to a military correction facility in Arlington. I had been handcuffed and shackled. I looked down at my wrists and ankles. The handcuffs and shackles were gone. We were slammed in the side by a large vehicle that pushed our SUV down a ravine. I escaped through the passenger door window. I was trying to scramble up the ravine slope when I got shot in my left leg. Did someone pick me up? I knew I was losing a lot of blood and getting woozy. I must have passed out then.

One adversary, Commander Logan, was now gone, I thought. However, he had been replaced by the President of the United States. And then there was the librarian, perhaps preparing to harvest its crop of humans at any time. I had trusted Commander Logan to help eradicate the librarian only to discover he and his Gruits were going to use the moon's Crystals to advance their Mandate; take over and control the United States and eventually the world. I was lost in thought when around the corner of the hallway Rosie entered the room. With a spreading smile on my face, I thought, ~What a pleasant surprise!~

~How are you feeling, Mike?~ Rosie asked.

~I feel really well. Was it all a dream or did I really get a bullet in my leg ?~

~You were shot by a gunman using a U.S. military rifle,~ Rosie responded. ~You lost most of your red fluid. We replaced the fluid before you ceased functioning.~

~When I realized I had been shot the blood was really coming out. The bullet must have severed a main vein or artery.~ I stepped off the bed. I walked to where Rosie was standing. I didn't feel any ill affects in my left leg at all. I shook Rosie's hand. ~I don't know how you did it, but thank you for saving my life!~ I could feel Rosie squeezing my hand. ~So where is Lumpy and James T?~ I asked.

~As you say,~ said Rosie, ~They are recharging. They will be joining us soon.~

~Rosie, where am I?~ I asked.

~You are in our lunar sanctuary,~ thought Rosie.

Something caught my eye. Outside the room's doorway, I could see a shadow. It appeared to be coming our way. Maybe Rosie was mistaken about Lumpy and James T. And then Satchmo entered the room! My eyes began welling up with tears as I rushed over, bent down and gave Satchmo a bear hug. ~It was you who lifted me up after I was shot and got me out of harm's way. But I don't understand, I thought your life ended in the hangar at Base S-4.~ I was so startled to see my old friend again.

~Access to other dimensions is an advantage when physical attention is called for,~ Satchmo thought.

Face to face, I looked into its eyes and gave it another huge hug. ~I am so glad to see you!~

~And I you,~ as Satchmo hugged me back.

~Mike, in this past day your arms and legs have been constrained, you experienced a horrendous vehicle accident and you were shot in the leg. Your life was in jeopardy until we managed a total transfusion of your body's red fluid. Do you need a 'recharging' period also? ~ asked Rosie.

~Considering your list of maladies, I feel really well,~ I thought.

Still concerned Rosie thought, ~Let us move to a more suitable room.~

As we walked to the doorway I looked down at Satchmo, put my hand on his shoulder and thought, ~Thanks again for saving me.~

Satchmo replied, ~You are most welcome.~

As I stood back up, the middle of my forehead slammed into

the edge of the door archway. "Geez!" I yelled. Momentarily stunned I realized I was bleeding from a gash on my forehead. Before the blood streamed into my eyes, I tried wiping it away. I looked around for a towel or cloth of some kind to use to put pressure on my wound. The room was completely bare. I wiped my forehead with my other hand and looked at it to determine how much I was bleeding. Both hands and all of my fingers were bright yellow. Rosie and Satchmo had stopped walking and were staring at me. ~Why are my hands and fingers bright yellow?!~ I yelled.

Rosie and Satchmo looked at one another and Rosie finally thought, ~It is because your body's red fluid is now yellow.~ Satchmo left the room.

~That is not an answer! Why is my blood bright yellow!?~ I demanded. By this time, my now yellow blood was running down the side of my face. Satchmo returned with a compress and handed it to me. I used one half of the compress to wipe my face and the other half to apply pressure to the wound.

Finally, Rosie explained, ~After Satchmo brought your body aboard Mr. Wizard, we took you to a different dimension to slow time and heal the wound in your leg. We also had to replace your red fluid. In that other dimension, there is no iron element. However, there is another metal element that works well in the hemoglobin that ab-sorbs and releases oxygen. Its color is yellow.~

What could I say? They saved my life by substituting what was left of my blood for another type of blood from a different dimension. I wondered, is that why I am feeling so well?

~Come back in the room and lie down. Satchmo, bring the epidermal adhesive,~ ordered Rosie.

Trying to be helpful I turned my head towards Rosie. ~If you turn your head the yellow liquid will cover your eyes. You will not be able to see,~ Rosie thought.

What did Rosie just think? ~What?! What did you just think?!~ I asked excitedly.

~You will not be able to see if you turn your head. The yellow liquid will block you vision,~ Rosie thought.

Of course! If you turn your head you can't see. Rosie's thought was the perfect analogy for what needed to take place! But how to accomplish it?

I laid back on the bed still compressing the wound on my forehead. Satchmo quickly returned with a new compress, and what looked like a roll of adhesive tape. Rosie wiped my blood away and applied the tape covering the two-inch gash on my forehead. ~That will stop the bleeding and heal the wound in a few moments. You must keep still,~ Rosie thought.

~While we have some time, you never told me about you guys visiting Ryan Logan's bedroom. What was the deal with that?~ I asked.

~As we have told you,~ Rosie thought, ~You were not ready when we visited you in your bedroom. We chose a replacement. Ryan Logan was ready, but ready for other reasons. We miscalculated with Ryan Logan. Even though several years went by, we stayed with our original choice. We calculated correctly with you.~

~Thanks for the explanation and having faith in me,~ I thought. ~Rosie, you just gave me an idea that may help alleviate my situation with the president and librarian, but it will require everyone's help and perhaps some other-worldly expertise. Do you think we can all meet somewhere in you lunar sanctuary soon so we can discuss this idea? And is Sundance and his crew close by? I would like them to join us.~

~Yes, I will summon Sundance. Your wound has healed. Follow us.~ I got up off of the bed and began following them. Then Rosie thought, ~Watch your head.~ I swear I heard Rosie chuckle.

As we walked down the narrow hallway I thought, ~Hey, Rosie, when we are finished with this meeting, I may want to go to the moon's Crystals. I have some unfinished business to attend to. I am going to need my clothes and, do you think you could explain to me how you unlock doors with your mind?~

I materialized in the Oval Office standing up in front of the president's desk. I was wearing the same clothes that Ryan had given me. The left pant leg was still covered in blood. The president was busy reading a typed letter on legal-sized paper. He finally looked up and visibly jumped in his chair when he saw me.

"Where did you come from?!" he shouted, "How did you get in here?!"

I looked down at him and calmly said, "I heard you weren't much of a marksman in the military, either. If I happen to appear in your bedroom some evening when you're asleep, I won't miss."

Trying to regain his composure, President Logan shifted in his chair and curtly asked, "What do you want?"

"What every American wants guaranteed by the United States Constitution; life, liberty, and the pursuit of happiness," I said firmly. "Leave my family and me alone!"

"You are a distinct threat to the United States' national security and an accomplice in treason against America!" he said authoritatively.

He hasn't called any guards yet, I thought. Either he wants to know what else I have planned or doesn't want to implicate himself in front of witnesses. "There will be a clear sky and full moon tonight in Washington, D.C. You may want to pay attention to that," I informed the president.

I walked over to the locked door that led to the outside of the Oval Office. This had better work, I thought. Following Rosie's instructions I tried opening the locked door with my mind. As I reached for the door handle I turned and looked at President Logan and said, "Have a nice night's sleep." I exited the Oval Office and walked into the mist.

20

According to United Kingdom lore, there are various ways of predicting the weather. For example, watching the behavior of wildlife can be useful:

> *If at dimpsey (twilight) the frogs do croakin',*
> *We'em be soon due a soakin'.*

Noticing the sky and surrounding environment is another tool for weather prediction:

> *When you can see the hills, it's going to rain.*
> *When you can't see the hills, it's raining.*

The behavior of plants is often used as a weather predictor:

> *When the dew is in the grass, rain will never come to pass.*
> *When grass is dry at mornings light, look for rain before night.*

Knowing what the weather will do can be accomplished by watching your pets' behavior:

> *If a cat washes its face o'er its ear*
> *'tis a sign the weather will be fine and clear.*

Time is also used to see what the weather will be like:

> *If Candlemas Day (February 2) is cold and clear,*
> *there'll be two winters in that year.*

And alcohol may be a factor in determining the weather. I made this one up myself:

> *There's nothing wrong with fog,*
> *if from whisky or a little grog.*

Tonight's weather throughout the celebrated county of Wiltshire in southwest England was a driving rain with rolling fog over the countryside. The locals may describe this weather as 'blowing a hooley' and 'throwing it down'. Two-thirds of the county lies on chalk; a soft, white, porous limestone. The chalk downland's landscape consists of rolling hills and small valleys. The highest point in Wiltshire is Milk Hill, a 968 foot high ridge just to the north of Salisbury Plain. There is not much to stop the fury of a north Atlantic storm crossing the county of Wiltshire.

The nickname for the locals in the county of Wiltshire is 'Moonrakers'. The story originated when smugglers would fool the local excise men by putting their alcohol in barrels and kegs, and then hide them in the village pond. To disguise the submerged contraband, they would form ripples by raking the water. They claimed they were trying to rake in a large round cheese visible on the pond's surface. It was really a reflection of a full moon. The excise men thought them simple yokels or just plain mad and left them alone. Tonight the ETs and I are going to become Moonrakers.

By the beam of my flashlight I watched small waves of rain-water form at the top of the sarsen stone and make their way down to the bottom of the huge stone structure. Even in the middle of this huge Atlantic storm sweeping through the Salisbury plain, Stonehenge was intriguing, mystifying, and beautiful. This evening the weather was foul with strong winds, cold temperatures, and a driving rain. All of the ETs stood in the middle of Stonehenge seemingly unaffected by the cruel elements of the storm. I had on my rain gear complete with a sou'wester. I hadn't worn rain gear like this since I was a deck-hand on the Washington State Ferries while working my way through college. Mr. Wizard was presumably located in a different time and dimension.

The direction of the storm was west by northwest. I took shelter between the east side of the tallest trilithon stone and part of the alter stone. I pointed the beam of the flashlight towards the heel stone. It was too dark to see, but I could make out all of the large sarsen stones and their lentils. What a dark, foreboding night; I hoped it doesn't impede our grand experiment.

I began thinking back to my meeting with the ETs in their lunar sanctuary earlier today. Everyone was present along with Sundance and its crew. Both spaceships were in attendance. I proposed a

grandiose plan that would hopefully bring a halt to the librarian and its scheme for humanity's fate. If the plan worked it could also put an end to the United States government's continued interest in my special talents. Surprisingly, during the presentation of my idea there was not one descending thought. Everyone was in agreement. So now it was up to the ETs to implement the timing, logistics, and details of this huge undertaking.

Late this afternoon we had traveled from the moon to Amesbury, a small town on the Salisbury Plains area, just a few miles from Stonehenge. I explained to the guys that I needed something to eat before implementing our plan. When we saw what the weather was like in Amesbury I asked them to drop me off at a store specializing in work clothes and rain gear. Then I could get something to eat and meet them at Stonehenge later.

I descended from Mr. Wizard in a small field next to a store featuring men's work wear. I dressed in my old clothes under the cover of Mr. Wizard. Fishing around in the bottom of the leather pouch, I found my wallet. As soon as the spacecraft left, I was soaked by the relentless rain. Fortunately, it was a short walk to the GMTS Workwear building. Getting help from an employee I purchased new clothes and rain gear. I asked the clerk where a nice pub was for dinner. Listening to her recommendation and directions, I hurriedly walked down Church Street to the Antrobus Arms Hotel.

It was a quaint, charming inn. Entering the lobby through a glass enclosure I shed my rain gear and hung it up on the hotel's hall tree. I followed a sign to the hotel's pub. No one was seated at the bar, so I took the stool on the end next to a window. The pounding rain on the window distorted the outside lights and scenery. It was also quickly becoming dusk. The barkeep came up and handed me a small menu. "Name's Robin. Wha' can I git fer ya, sir?" Without looking at the menu, I ordered Shepard's Pie and a pint of Guinness. I was famished! While I was waiting for my Guinness I turned around to view the small hotel pub. On the opposite wall was a little fireplace with a small fire smoking and crackling inside its box. There were four ornate wood tables surrounded by leather-back chairs with arms. The floor was dark oak. Then a picture frame caught my eye on the fireplace mantel. There was no picture in it, but a saying: 'In defense of alcohol, I've done some pretty stupid things completely sober, too.' I chuckled a little and thought, I hoped tonight wasn't going to be one of them.

I'm not a big fan of lamb, but the Shepard's Pie was delicious, especially washed down with a pint of Guinness. I paid for my dinner and asked Robin if he would call a cab for me. When the cab driver came into the bar to fetch me, I went with him out to the lobby. I put my rain clothes on and walked out into the weather. In the impending dark of night there were two cabs outside the hotel and they looked exactly the same: black color, fenders, rectangular chrome grill, similar hood over the engine and squared-off back trunks. The cab driver and I walked up to the closest cab and he asked, "So no luggage tonight, sir?"

"Just me and my flashlight," I said holding it up. He reached for the handle to open the door for me, but it was locked. He tried again, then realized it was not his cab. "My god," he said stunned. "I don't even know which one is my own cab. My apologies, sir." He directed me to the proper one. Once seated inside, I told him my destination. He looked at me in the rear view mirror and gave an odd look. "Yes, sir," he said as we headed out. "Sorry about the cab mix up. You know, a few night's ago I was at a friend's party. He has a new place and we are expected to take our shoes off in the home's foyer before entering. Well, after a few hours I said my goodbyes, put my shoes on and went home. The next morning I go to put my shoes back on and they are way too big. I wore the wrong pair of shoes home."

After a good laugh and a couple of other stories we were getting close to Stonehenge. We took A360 off of A303, took a right at a roundabout and arrived at the Stonehenge visitor's gravel parking lot. "Sir, I usually don't say anything, but Stonehenge is closed to visitors this evening. There won't be another soul here."

"I don't know if they have souls, but I won't be alone. Thank you, I'll be fine," I said.

"Would you like me to hang around for your return trip back to Amesbury?"

"That won't be necessary," I said as I paid my fee. "Thanks for the ride and entertainment." I stepped out into the weather, adjusted my sou'wester and closed the cab door.

~Mike. Mike? Mike!~ Startled, I came out of my daydreaming. Rosie thought, ~We must be outside the sarsen ring in a few moments.~ I turned the flashlight beam around the sarsens until I saw where Rosie and the rest of them had moved. They were just to the north of the two sarsens with a lentil on top. Oh, great. They were standing in the brunt of the storm. I strode over and joined them with my head down as a shield to the storm's wind and rain. I wiped some rain off of my face.

As I stood next to Rosie and the guys something incredible began to happen. Each sarsen stone began to glow a pale green color at their base. Even the Q and R holes where sarsen stones once stood thousands of years ago began to glow. The green glow began to climb each sarsen stone to their tops. Even where the sarsens used to be the green glow took the shape of the original stones. Real or fabricated, all thirty sarsen stones composing the outer ring of Stonehenge were now present. The lintels, the stones on top connecting all of the sarsens together began to take shape, connecting to each other and glowing green.

~Rosie, where is Mr. Wizard right now?~ I asked.

~Mr. Wizard is here and Mr. Wizard is there.~

I gave Rosie a puzzled look to which it responded, ~We shall see if the sarsen stones perform as predicted.~

In the light of the green glow all of the guys, even Sundance's crew were staring at Stonehenge and the sarsen stones. We all watched for something to happen. Then Rosie pointed to the bottoms of the stones. A dark green ring about two feet in height formed on each one. The ring quickly moved up to the top of the lentils. As it did, there was an audible crackling sound similar to static electricity. And then a huge circular impulse of green light exploded into the night sky heading straight up. It sounded like a musical note from a muted bass saxophone. The repercussion of the green light's impulse sent me back and down on my butt. Once again I wiped rain from my face as I stood back up and braced myself for the next impulse. It wasn't but a moment until the next impulse of other-worldly energy was sent skyward. The outer circle of Stonehenge stones was sending a circular energy impulse into the earth's atmosphere about every three seconds. It was an awe-inspiring spectacle.

One of the qualities of the sarsen, lentil, and trilithon stones is that they are loaded with quartz crystals. At our meeting with the ETs in their lunar sanctuary earlier today we discussed certain attributes that quartz crystals possess. When subjected to an electric current they vibrate at a rate of 32,000 hertz. Conversely, when quartz crystals are subjected to mechanical pressure, they create an electric current. The size of the stones at Stonehenge range from four meters to nine meters high. Their weights are twenty-four to thirty-five tons. All are mostly composed of silica and quartz crystals. What if we were able to generate an electric current powerful enough to run through the stones of Stonehenge? Could we create a massive electric current to do something unimaginable ?

After some thoughtful discussion the ETs suggested using an energy source from another dimension utilizing an entirely different energy spectrum. They indicated Mr. Wizard's expertise would make the energy source more manageable, but also more powerful. From all indications this evening, that was the correct choice.

~How is it doing, Rosie?~ I asked.

~It is performing with our perceived specifications.~

Mmmm, our perceived specifications, I thought. Earlier today at the meeting I reminded the ETs of my first visit inside the moon's Crystals. I chose Stonehenge to view and study. When I directed the hexagonal plate back in time to witness a completed Stonehenge, the stone structure reminded me of a large speaker from an old hi-fi stereo cabinet. It looked very similar to some kind of amplifier.

Stonehenge has been proven to possess extraordinary acoustics. Using lasers and 3-D printer technology, scientists from the University of Salford in Manchester, constructed a 112th scale-model of Stonehenge. Placed in a sound room the model exhibited high quality reverberations of sound, song, chants, and speech. The full-scale model of Stonehenge in Maryhill, Washington, underwent similar testing and found the same results. The acoustics of songs, chants, and speech were greatly amplified even though it is completely outside with no walls or ceiling. Imagine people of the neolithic period experiencing this at Stonehenge. It truly could have been a magical and spiritual structure in their eyes.

As Mike Parker Pearson suggested in his book 'Stonehenge, A New Understanding', *the designers of that first Stonehenge had big plans: It wasn't just a unification of people and places, drawing bluestones from an ancestral place of power in Wales, but also a unification of the entire cosmos--the earth, the sun, and the moon.*

The guys and I were attempting to take it one step further to include not just the earth, sun, and moon but the stars and heavens, too. We were attempting to use Stonehenge for what may have been its intended original purpose--an energy amplifier! If Stonehenge was ever struck by lightening in neolithic times, the dead that were buried there may have been sent to the heavens via an electrical impulse through the night sky!

21

As energy impulses were sent skyward one after the other from Stonehenge, Rosie looked at me. ~There is a concern.~

I turned and faced Rosie. ~What is it? I asked. This didn't sound good.

~Sundance's craft, located between the earth and the moon cannot direct the energy impulses in the intended direction to the target area. The energy vortex that the impulses are going through is too wide. It must be narrowed and made more firm,~ Rosie explained.

~Can we do that from here somehow~? I asked

~Mr. Wizard will try and divert a proportional amount of the other-dimensional energy to the trilithon horseshoe enabling the vortex to straighten and become rigid. This should allow Sundance's craft to capture and direct the energy impulses to the intended location. Shall we proceed?~ asked Rosie.

~Please inform both crafts to immediately implement the alternate plan!~ I thought strongly. Geez, I hope this works. Now all of our planning depends on the success of this additional manipulation.

The trilithon horseshoe, located towards the entrance of Stonehenge, began to glow with the pale green light from the bottom of the stones to the top. I braced myself for the energy impulse to explode from the trilithon horseshoe and into space. We watched and waited for several seconds. Nothing was happening. ~Rosie, is there a problem?~ I asked.

~The end of the trilithon horseshoe needs to be closed so the circuit between the trilithon stones can be complete,~ Rosie thought.

~How can we do that? We certainly can't drag any stones to the open end of the horseshoe to complete the circuit,~ I thought.

~Satchmo, Lumpy, James T, myself, and Sundance and his crew can close the circuit. Stonehenge is grounded in chalk. We believe no ill harm will come to us. By holding hands we will form a line while touching the end stones and completing the circuit,~ Rosie explained.

Some foreign energy source from another dimension flowing through the ETs bodies is going to be safe? I thought ~Hey guys, is this such a good idea? Isn't there an alternate plan we can use?~

As I thought my concerns they marched out to the ends of the trilithon horseshoe and began forming a line from one end of the horseshoe opening to the other. James T was at the far end touching the end stone and Sundance was on the near end with all the other ETs inside forming a straight line. They all clasped hands and stretched out to touch each end stone to close the circuit. To my horror, their arms and bodies weren't long enough to complete the circuit. It appeared they were about four feet short! All at once every ET head turned and looked straight at me.

~NO!~ I shouted. ~I can't help complete a circuit of some energy form from a different dimension! There's got to be another way that doesn't involve me!~

Just then, the rain stopped. Directly overhead the clouds momentarily cleared revealing a bright, full moon. The cheese we needed to rake in, I thought. Geez. I walked over to the ETs line and joined next to Sundance. As I held its hand the moon disappeared behind the clouds and the rain began again. I looked over at James T. He was touching the trilithon stone while holding Lumpy's hand. Reluctantly, I put my right hand on the other trilithon stone and completed the circuit.

"Ohhhh!" I exclaimed as my body began to pulse and my eyes widened. The hair inside my sou'wester stood straight up. Before I lost track of time and space, a small smile formed on my face.

~Mike, Mike. Please wake up. Mike!~ I was lying on my back next to the trilithon stone I had been touching. My eyes were closed. I didn't want to get up quite yet. I don't smoke, but a cigarette might be satisfying right now. Finally I sat up on my elbows and thought, ~Rosie, is everyone all right?~

~Yes,~ Rosie thought.

~Were we successful?~ I asked.

~We were successful.~

~How long did it take?~

~Approximately ninety minutes,~ was Rosie's answer.

With a smile still on my face Rosie held out its hand and I took it. Rosie pulled me up and I gave it a hug. I looked around and everyone had formed a circle around me. Starting with Sundance I shook everyone's hand, gave each a hug and thanked them all. The terrible nightmare that Kate and I had experienced during the last few days was hopefully going to be over.

The knocking on the bedroom door was soft, but deliberate. "Who is it?" the president asked loudly. He readjusted the .32 caliber pistol in his right hand putting his index finger on the trigger.

"Ken, sir," answered the president's chief of staff.

The president, relieved, said, "Come in, Ken." The president looked at the clock on the night stand. It was 3:37 a.m. He hadn't gotten much sleep this evening. The interruption was a welcome diversion to what was on his mind. Ken opened the door and entered the president's bedroom. He noticed there was a glowing night light next to the president's bed; rather unusual.

"What is it, Ken?" The president saw that Ken had a pair of binoculars in his right hand.

"I think you should see this, sir. But you need to go out on the balcony," informed Ken. This was odd, the president thought. Usually Ken would verbally give me a full report and then hand me a written version.

President Logan got out of bed leaving the pistol under the sheets. As he put on his bathrobe, Ken couldn't help but notice the outline of the gun under the bed sheets. "This way, Mr. President," as Ken led the president from his bedroom into the private sitting room.

"This is highly unusual, Ken," the president said. There was a tone of anxiety in his voice.

"Just wait, Mr. President," answered Ken.

Ken opened the door to the Truman Balcony and stepped outside. President Logan followed him onto the balcony that overlooked the South Lawn. The air was crisp and refreshing. The lawn was clearly visible from the light of the full moon. When they reached the railing, Ken handed the binoculars to the president. "Take a look at the moon using the binoculars, sir," instructed Ken. The president put the binoculars to his eyes, adjusted the setting and stared at the moon. Something wasn't quit right, the president thought. He couldn't put his finger on what appeared to be unusual.

"Something is different, Ken. What am I looking at?" the president asked.

"You are looking at the far side of the moon, the dark side," Ken informed the president.

The president turned to Ken and asked, "How the hell did this happen?!" The president was incredulous. The implications were astonishing, he thought.

"I have been in contact with NASA, sir," Ken said. "Nobody knows, so far."

Then President Logan began thinking back to what McAlister had told him in the Oval Office yesterday. What did he say, the president thought?

"There will be a clear sky and full moon tonight here in Washington, D.C. You may want to pay attention to that."

President Logan took one more look at the moon through the binoculars. He handed them back to Ken and said, "When you get back to your office, please inform the Department of Justice and the Central Intelligence Agency that we are no longer interested in Michael McAlister."

22

The librarian was in a foul mood. It was hissing, bubbling, and emitting a horrid odor more than usual. By nature, its race of beings were vile, contemptible, and vicious. For the librarian, the grand experiment was over. The moon, the huge data gathering device had turned 180 degrees. The array underneath the moon's surface that collected the human data was now pointed towards outer space. It was worthless to the librarian. And there wasn't anything it could do to remedy the situation. Billions of years wasted, it thought. I was so close.

It wasn't a librarian really, but more of a gardener watching its plants growing to harvest. Or it was a rancher keeping track of its herd. However, the librarian was going to miss out on the most satisfying part of its tenure in the moon; that of butcher. Just a while longer and the humans would have been ready to preserve; billions of cylindrical tubes all containing an earthling buried beneath the earth's surface.

Soon though, the librarian would be making the journey home. It had started preparations for the trip after the moon shifted position. One lesson learned; do not engage in the species that will eventually become your food source. I may be disciplined on my return home for this colossal failure. Upon this thought, the librarian's mood worsened.

I had been exhausted after our Stonehenge adventure and slept a few hours on Mr. Wizard's deck. Just waking up, I saw that we were slowly approaching the Crystals inside the moon. Now that the moon had been turned around to the dark side facing earth, would that make a difference in retrieving Kate from 1989? We may have made a mistake, I thought. I had this gut feeling that maybe the ETs and I had really screwed things up. Disembarking Mr. Wizard, we all walked and stood just outside the wall that surrounds the Crystals. I looked at Rosie and it thought, ~Proceed, please.~

I got dressed and put the leather pouch strap over my head and on my left shoulder. My hand went on the closest Crystal. As always, I was transported to a slate gray pathway and taken inside. Once inside one of the Crystal's corridors I engaged a hexagonal crystal plate, found the best time for my return to Ponderosa Estates and engaged.

I materialized by the barn. Breathing a sigh of relief I thought, thank god it worked. I saw young Mike walking towards his log home across the parking area. As if sensing me, he stopped and turned around and looked at me. "Well, are you leaving or what?" he asked.

"What?" I said, puzzled.

"We just said good bye," young Mike said. "I thought you'd be long gone by now."

"Oh, wow. You know, I haven't exactly perfected this traveling back in time thing yet," I explained. "I think I've actually been gone about three days."

Just then Kate and young Kate came around the barn from the horse stalls. "When are you leaving?" Kate asked. "I'd thought you'd already be gone."

"Well, as I just explained to Mike here, I'm not always precise about coming and going in time. Really, I've been gone about three days my time," I said. "Before I tell you about the last few days, I want to show you something. Let's go into the kitchen for a moment."

We all walked into the log home and I got a paring knife from the knife holder in the kitchen. With everyone watching, I pricked the end of my left thumb. I gave it a little squeeze as bright yellow blood oozed out. Surprised at the color, Kate asked, "What is that?!"

"Let's go out to the front porch, get comfy, and I'll tell you all about my last three days," I said.

After sitting down on the porch I began talking about my Mars adventures; being poisoned by certain Martians and discovering the librarian's true intentions. After that came Commander Logan's Gruits' meeting and eventual arrest. I described being handcuffed and shackled by the President of the United States and then shot by a presidential sniper. To save my life, I explained that the ETs took me to another dimension and gave me a blood transfusion with a yellow element replacing the iron in my blood. Finally, I recounted how the ETs and I

put a half-twist on the moon using Stonehenge as an energy amplifier. That half-twist rendered the librarian's plans for humans useless and hopefully convinced the president to leave Kate and me alone.

"I think Kate and I can finally go home," I concluded. Young Kate and Mike and Kate just looked at me with expressions of disbelief for several moments. Kate came over to my chair, put her arms around me and gave me one of the best kisses ever. Eventually young Mike exclaimed, "Unbelievable! Really, all of that in just three days? You couldn't make all of that up, it has to be true! Really unbelievable! We're so glad you came back alive and in one piece. Hey, you said you'd bring me back something from the future."

"I did. I brought you three things," I said proudly as I reached into the leather pouch. I handed young Mike the first item. "Here's a bottle of Coke Zero." Then I put a rock, about the size of a walnut, in his other hand.

"A rock? I've got some of these right here in our driveway," exclaimed young Mike.

"Not just any rock," I said. "When I was on Mars with the ETs, I palmed it and put it in the pouch."

"A Martian rock," young Mike said quizzically, as he turned it around and around examining it. "How cool is that? Thanks Mike."

"And here's the last thing." I handed young Mike a framed photograph.

Young Mike looked and looked at the photo for several seconds and finally asked, "What is this all about?"

"That is the first time I met the ETs. I wasn't aware that Kate had taken a picture of us."

With a smile on his face, young Mike said, "Well, for sixty I still look pretty good from behind."

Kate thought, ~How did you get that photo? Did you go home before you came here?~

~Technically yes,~ I thought. ~But I was asleep aboard Mr. Wizard at the time and the ETs agreed to get it and the Coke Zero for me.~

We all said our thank yous and good byes. I stuck out my arm and Kate took it. Then she and I walked into the mist and disappeared.

Safely onboard Mr. Wizard we began our journey up to the moon's surface and home to Pine Creek. Having told everyone of my exploits during the past three days, I began to realize the scope of those events. I will be so glad to be going back to our home living a normal life and off of the world stage, I thought.

Whether a coincidence or planned event, the librarian's departure from the Crystals and the moon coincided with Mike, Kate, and the ETs leaving the moon. Sensing them the librarian, in a last vicious, vindictive act lashed out to Kate and Mike's minds erasing all and any memories of the extraterrestrials, the moon, the Crystals, and itself. It was like a whip unleashed taking those memories away. Immediately, Kate and Mike both crumpled to the deck of Mr. Wizard. They laid there unconscious.

Rosie, Lumpy, Satchmo, and James T looked at one another and then looked down at Kate and Mike. They all knew what had just taken place. Worse yet, they all knew what they had to do.

23

The ETs and Mr. Wizard began their descent to Pine Creek and Kate and Mike's home. Their craft slowed to a stop and hovered over its familiar position just above the front lawn at the McAlister residence. Rosie, Satchmo, and Lumpy exited Mr. Wizard while James T lowered Mike and Kate into their awaiting arms. The springer spaniels, Bill and Sammie, came running out of the garage to greet them. The familiar scent of their beloved owners was a welcome relief. They were jumping, barking, howling, and sniffing the unconscious bodies. Bill and Sammie knew something wasn't quite right. But they were overjoyed that Mike and Kate were home, safe with the ETs taking care of them.

They carried Mike and Kate into their home. Carefully, they placed them on the living room's carpeted floor. Retrieving clothes from the bedroom closet, they began dressing both of the McAlisters. As they worked Rosie, Lumpy, Satchmo, and James T shared a single thought. They had lost a friend; friends, actually. For billions of years they did not have a friend nor emotional feelings about friendship, until now. And today their friends were gone. Memories of all the adventures they shared were taken away by the vengeful librarian. And there was nothing they could do about it; helpless and hopeless. Occasionally they would stop and look at one another wondering what this odd feeling was that they were sharing. They had never experienced loss before. It did not feel good to them.

The ETs finished their task. Mike was seated upright in the oak rocker while Kate was laid on the leather couch with a pillow carefully placed under her head. All the while the dogs were licking Kate and Mike's faces, arms, and hands in excitement of their owner's return. They will wake up soon, thought Rosie. We must be going. Each ET touched the right shoulders of Mike and Kate before leaving the house. Bill and Sammie followed them out to the front lawn where Mr. Wizard was waiting. Once again, each ET petted the dogs one last time. They slowly boarded their craft. Mr. Wizard took its time leaving the Pine Creek area.

I woke up and heard Kate in the kitchen. I looked around the living room. That's weird, I thought. I took a nap and in the rocking chair? "Hey Kate, what time is it?"

"Almost four, so you finally woke up?" asked Kate.

I got out of the rocker and walked into the kitchen. "Boy, that was odd. I hardly ever take a nap," I said.

Kate looked at me and said with a smile, "Here's something even odder. Look how you're dressed."

I looked down my front. I was wearing an orange t-shirt advertising a saloon in King Salmon, Alaska. Black slacks and brown dress shoes rounded out my outfit. What was going on here, I thought?

"What's the matter, Kate. You don't like brown dress shoes with black slacks?"

"Well, I just woke up a few minutes ago myself. I was sleeping on the couch. Look at what I'm wearing, an old cotton summer dress from twenty years ago. And my undies were on backwards," Kate said with a questioning tone.

"What on earth were we doing when we were asleep?" I asked suspiciously. "I don't even remember what I did all day, whatever that was. It must have been pretty strenuous for me to take a nap. Well, I'm going to change clothes. I think the lawn needs mowing."

"I'm thawing out some hamburger. You want to grill burgers for dinner tonight?" Kate asked.

"Yeah, sure. Sounds great. I'm starving!"

I went into the bedroom and changed into some work clothes and then walked outside. Geez, I thought, look how tall the grass is. Yes, the lawn definitely needed mowing. Just then the dogs came running around the corner of the garage barking, howling, and jumping up and down on me.

"Guys, guys, you know better. Down, down!" I knelt down on the front lawn while Bill and Sammie couldn't get enough of my attention. What has gotten into them? I tried calming them with mild success. Then Bill, all excited that I was down at their level, scratched my arm with his right front paw.

"Okay, okay!" I lowered my voice. "Sit, sit, and calm down." It seemed to be working. They were finally becoming manageable. I petted and stroked each of their heads. Then I saw my arm that Bill had scratched. A bright yellow liquid was coming out instead of blood.

"Bill, let me see your paw." I picked it up, turned it and took a look. There wasn't anything to see. I wiped the yellow liquid off with my other hand. The oozing stuff was slowing down until it finally quit. Now what was the deal with that, I thought?

The grilled burgers tasted great and the evening proceeded without incident. I decided not to tell Kate yet about the bright yellow liquid. One mystery today was plenty. We finished the day watching a rerun of Friends. Funny thing, we never watched Friends when it was current. But now we couldn't watch enough of them. When the show finished, we were in bed by ten and out by five after. Just before I fell asleep, I wondered what tomorrow would bring after the strange events of today. Hopefully, it was going to be a normal day tomorrow… zzzz.

24

Early the next morning I woke up and noticed a strange light coming from outside the master bedroom window. It was pale green and pulsating. Kate was awake too, and saw the green light. "Mike, what is that?" she asked.

"Don't know," I said. "I'll take a look." As I got up I noticed the clock on the night stand. It was 2:33 a.m. At least it wasn't 3:33 a.m.

I opened the bedroom door and walked down the hallway to the foyer. Coming through the windows the pulsating light caste an eerie greenish glow in the house. As I looked around I saw the numbers 188843 suspended above the table in the foyer. It too, was pulsating. Wow, that's weird. What the hell is going on here? Well, one thing at a time. Where's this green light coming from? I walked over to the front door. On tip-toes, I looked out the front door window.

Acknowledgments

Well, my editor quit in a huff a few months ago. I thought wives were supposed to be helpful and supportive. Actually, my lovely wife Chris, read each chapter as they became available. She helped me sort out bad grammar, spelling errors, and stuff that didn't even make sense. But you can still blame her if you find something that needs to be fixed.

Grandson Jaden suggested that the Martians' skin color should be red. Really? Okay, I'll give that one to him. Mayan, my granddaughter, said something to me the last time I saw her in Charlotte, NC. I put what she had said in the book. We'll see if she can spot it. They are seventeen and fifteen year old high school students so they have other things on their mind.

Phyllis Emmert once again agreed to illustrate Dark Side if I promised this would be the last book. Aren't her illustrations great? Hey, and what about that librarian? Does it remind you of some of the librarians you've dealt with in the past? To be fair though, most are extremely nice and helpful. You can see her paintings and art work at phyllisemmert.com.

Lastly, Gray Dog Press aka Minuteman Press. It was so easy dealing with Stefan and Bob. Bob came up with the book cover design and helped me through the publication process with IngramSpark. A big thanks to Stefan and Bob.

Oh, and hertz means 'per second'.